PCH

Deported

A PORT CITY HIGH NOVEL

SHANNON FREEMAN

SADDLEBACK
PUBLISHING

High School High

Taken

Deported

The Public Eye

www.sdlback.com

Copyright ©2014 by Saddleback Educational Publishing
All rights reserved. No part of this book may be reproduced in any form or by any means, electronic or mechanical, including photocopying, recording, scanning, or by any information storage and retrieval system, without the written permission of the publisher. SADDLEBACK EDUCATIONAL PUBLISHING and any associated logos are trademarks and/or registered trademarks of Saddleback Educational Publishing.

ISBN-13: 978-1-62250-039-0
ISBN-10: 1-62250-039-3
eBook: 978-1-61247-682-7

Printed in Guangzhou, China
NOR/1113/CA21302125

18 17 16 15 14   1 2 3 4 5

ACKNOWLEDGMENTS

Thank you to my husband for being my go-to when there aren't enough hours in the day to write. You are priceless and tireless when it comes to supporting me and my dream. Not many authors have a full marketing team at their home. I am so blessed to have you on my side. When I have writer's block, you are the one I turn to. Thank you for keeping my stories fresh and accurate ... my hardest critic, my biggest supporter ... I love you.

Thank you to Nana (Carolyn Warrick) and Mall Mall (Deborah Freeman). I couldn't have done this without your support. When there's a deadline, you jump in there and watch my babies. For my three mini-people, Kingston, Addyson, and Brance, thank you for being understanding and sharing your mother with the world. You are truly my heart.

Rochelle Jenkins, Felisha Collins, Shannon Richard, Qiana Settles, Evette Rodgers, Tia Huebel, Jennifer Osgood, and Diasheena Gabriel ... you are my sisters. You keep me laughing even when life gets stressful. I hope that I am to you what you are to me—a gift and blessing from God. Love you.

—Shannon Freeman

DEDICATION

To my future aspiring authors (you know who you are). I hope I inspire you as much as you inspire me. I want to be the first in line at your book signing. Never stop writing.

Prologue

It had been an amazing summer—barbeques, swimming, vacations. Who could ask for more? When the flyers were circulated that the first annual Back-to-School Blowout was being thrown by Port City officials, everyone was super-excited. Marisa, Shane, and Brandi had been preparing for two weeks for the Hawaiian-themed party. They ordered the cutest flowered outfits online and made their own grass skirts. They each found leis that complimented their clothes perfectly.

Now they were at Mari's house getting ready for the event.

"I am not ready to see everybody," Brandi announced. It had only been a couple of months since Brandi had been abducted by Steven, a demented childhood friend. In his mind, he thought he was saving her from her family and friends. But he hurt her more than they ever could. She was still trying to heal and move beyond the terror.

"You are going to be fine," Marisa said as her reflection met Brandi's in the tall mirror. "Plus look at all of the support you have. It won't just be me and Shane. Trent and Ashton will be with us too. You know they have your back." They had only met Trent and Ashton last semester. Marisa had fallen in love with Trent, but Trent and Ashton had become like brothers to Brandi. They had helped rescue her from Steven and had remained supportive throughout the summer, taking her to cheerleading practice and calling to check in.

"Girl, quit trippin'," Shane said as she came out of the restroom. She had pulled her hair into a bun on top of her head. Her bangs framed her golden sun-kissed face.

"I feel self conscious, like I shouldn't be showing so much skin. I don't want to bring attention to myself. I'm going to let the knot out of this shirt," Brandi decided.

"You will do no such thing," Shane said. "Show off all that chocolate honey. You look good." And she did. The contrast of the Hawaiian colors on Brandi's dark skin made her look like an African queen.

"Argh, I don't know. I should have gotten the other dress like Mari's."

"Girl, I'm about to tie this one in a knot on the side too. I have to show a little leg," Marisa said.

"That's more than a little leg. You're almost six feet tall, woman. That's a whole lotta leg," Shane said, laughing.

"That's why Trent loves me. He needs all this woman by his side. Hey, he's texting me. They're outside. Mama, we are leaving!" she yelled.

"*Mi hija*, let me get a picture before you go."

"Mama, Trent is outside."

"Well, tell Trent to come inside," Mrs. Maldonado said. Marisa had really been on her mother about learning to speak English. She had been in classes all summer, and it was finally helping. She was so proud of her.

"He can't tonight, Mama. We have tickets for the first barge ride, so we have to be on time. Just get us girls. We'll take pictures for you when we get there."

"Now you know I'll get my photography on, Mrs. M," Shane said.

"Okay, okay, *uno foto*," Mrs. Maldonado said, snapping their picture. They each gave her a kiss on the cheek and ran to meet Trent and Ashton.

When they got outside, they were shocked. "Is this the Hummer SUT?" Shane asked Trent.

"The girl knows her vehicles," Ashton said, jumping in the back to let Marisa sit up front with Trent.

"Yes, sir. They don't even make these anymore. Where did you find this, Trent?" she asked.

"My parents got it for me. I'm leaving for college next year, so it's an early graduation present."

"Don't remind me," Marisa said, giving him a kiss.

"Oh, get a room already," Shane said playfully.

"No, those purity rings are stopping any room action," Ashton said, laughing at his friend. The girls all wore the purity rings that Shane's sister, Robin, had given them when she found out that she was pregnant. She didn't want them to make the same mistakes that she had made.

"Heeeey," Brandi and Shane said simultaneously, punching Ashton in the arm.

"You should be happy you're with girls who are pure."

"Yeah, lucky us," Ashton said sarcastically, getting another punch from the girls. "Ow! Next time, I'm hitting back."

As they pulled up to the seawall, Trent rolled the top back on the Hummer. They took their place in line with the other juniors and seniors who wanted to flaunt their new vehicles. Everybody had their music blasting. Texas rap could be heard everywhere. Young Dub and anybody else signed with Third Coast Records blared through various sound systems.

"Yo, I'm standing up! Let's see what's popping," Shane said excitedly.

"Trade seats with me, Ashton. I wanna be by my girls." Ashton and Marisa jumped out of the truck so that the girls could be together in the back.

Standing up in that huge Hummer let them tower over everyone. They could see the whole party from one end of the seawall to the other. The boats and barges had been pulled to the docks and decorated with lights. Each boat had its own party. Some of them even went out for a brief cruise along the port. You could feel the energy of the crowd; it was electric.

Trent and Ashton hung out of the car windows as various girls strolled along the seawall. The girls hollered their names like they were stars. Well, in Port City they were stars. Their basketball skills had earned them some fame. Trent was impressed that Marisa never got jealous when girls threw themselves at him. She was so confident, and that was attractive to him.

"Ooh, I wanna go to that party," Shane said. "The people are wearing masks and everything."

"I'll pass," Brandi said abruptly.

"Stop being like that, B. Loosen up," Shane said, nudging her.

"I have to be able to see people's faces. I'll always think that everybody is Steven. Never mind, I can tell I can't make you understand."

"Hey, don't worry about Steven. I'll take care of that fool," Ashton said, kissing his muscles.

"Seriously, I'm tired of seeing your muscles or lack thereof," Shane said, teasing him. "Put those little twigs away."

"Sure you are. Just like I'm tired of looking at your beautiful face," Ashton said, making Shane blush. He was a hopeless flirt.

They decided to head straight to the food carts along the seawall and load up on barbeque, roasted corn, funnel cakes, and frosty fresh-squeezed lemonade before going to their ship. Their party boat was set to sail in thirty minutes, enough time to eat, drink, and get on the boat.

As soon as they pulled away from the dock, the DJ started to spin Young Dub's newest song, "BALLIN ... But I Don't Play." They went straight to the dance floor and never left for the entire boat ride.

The next boat that they chose was super fun. The theme was murder-mystery. The banner on the side of the boat read "Who dun it?" Brandi solved the mystery in record time and won a backpack full of school supplies.

By two a.m. they had seen all of their friends, the basketball team, and even some of their teachers out having a good time. They called it a night. The traffic was horrible leaving the seawall, but they finally made it out of the tangle of cars and onto the highway. By the time they arrived at Marisa's house, the girls were exhausted and ready for bed.

"Well ... last weekend before we go back to school," Trent said.

"Right," they said, getting out of the car.

"I hate to see summer go," Marisa added.

"I hate to see you go," Trent said, giving her a kiss.

"Dude." Ashton tried to stop him from getting too mushy.

"On that note, I'm out," Shane said, hugging her new big brothers.

Brandi did the same. "Love y'all! Call us and be safe."

CHAPTER 1

Marisa

The smell of chorizo, eggs, and homemade tortillas filled the Maldonado home. "I think I'm going to move in if your mom keeps making homemade tortillas," Shane said, turning over with her eyes still shut.

"Shoot, it's the chorizo that I smell. My mouth is watering over here," Brandi said. "But I don't want to move."

"I'm sick of chorizo and eggs, for real. I'm just having juice, and I don't want to hear anything about it," Marisa said, knowing her friends wanted her to eat.

Shane opened her eyes enough to peek at Marisa. "You need to eat. You're going to fly away."

"As long as I fly to Milan, I'm okay with that. And I do eat, you know that."

"Well, I'm about to eat right now," Brandi said, going to the bathroom to brush her teeth. "Y'all can talk about it. I'ma be about it."

The night before had taken all of their energy. Not only had they danced until they ached, but the excitement had been draining too. That last summer bash had marked the beginning of the end of summer, and that meant school would start, which was depressing. It was always sad for them to see summer end and leave behind sunbathing by the pool, staying up late, and being home alone while your parents were at work.

"Hey, I'm down for food. Don't leave me," Shane whined as she tried to shake off the previous night.

"You know the way to the kitchen," Brandi told her as she left the bedroom.

Shane huffed. She hurried to the bathroom to make herself presentable.

"*Buenos dias*, Mrs. M," Brandi said, entering the kitchen.

"Good morning to you too, Brandi. You hungry?"

"Yes, ma'am," she said, smiling. Mrs. Maldonado brought her a plate of chorizo and eggs, some corn tortillas, homemade salsa—made with fresh tomatoes from their garden—and a large glass of orange juice. "I swear I'm moving in. Stop spoiling me."

"Anytime, mi hija. You know you are always welcome."

"Y'all started without me," Shane said, looking down at Brandi as she ate her breakfast.

"Here's a plate, honey," Mrs. Maldonado told her. "Mari, what do you want?"

"Not chorizo, Mama. I have to watch

my weight. Orange juice and fruit will be fine," she said, scooping strawberries into a bowl.

"How about some plain egg whites?" her mother asked.

"That sounds good."

"Get outta my seat," Romero said as he walked into the kitchen, thumping Shane on the head.

She playfully jumped at him in retaliation. "Don't play with me, Romero. Where are your sisters?" she asked.

"Sleepin'. Same place I would be if your big mouth was at home."

"You better leave her alone," Marisa said, threatening her little brother.

"Um-hm," Brandi mumbled with her mouth full of food. "You better be glad I'm eating."

"That's not new," he started to say, but they attacked him before he could get the words out. "Okay, okay," he said as they carried him to the den.

"Marisa, you girls stop! You're going to hurt your brother!" They could hear Mrs. Maldonado yelling at them.

"Never, Mama! He asked for it!"

"Y'all are gonna get it," he warned them. They had him pinned. Marisa had his legs, Brandi his arms, and Shane was in charge of tickle torture. He laughed until he hurt. "I can't stand girls," he announced when they let him up.

"Yeah, right! You love us," Brandi said breathlessly.

"And you can have your little seat," Shane said, pushing him in the head.

"Yo, Mari, you think Trent can take me and Sam to Seawall Sunday?"

"Um ... no. Trent doesn't want to hang out with two eighth graders. Besides, you want to go with him because he has that Hummer."

"He got that SUT? I'm calling him myself."

"No you're not! Come back here!" she

yelled, but she knew he would call and Trent wouldn't refuse. That was just how he was.

"Cool! I'll be ready. And don't call Mari. She's a hater," she heard him say.

"I am not!" she yelled.

"Thanks for breakfast, Mrs. M," Shane said, kissing her on the cheek.

"Yeah, it was so good," Brandi told her.

"I'm just glad to feed everyone. Marisa barely eats."

"Mari, we're out. Robin's here," Shane told her.

"Okay, I'll call you later."

Marisa relaxed and caught up on her *novellas* as she waited for Trent to show up. The days seemed to be flying by; school was tomorrow. She heard a knock on the door and ran to meet Trent, but it was only Samuel Rodriguez, her little brother's best friend.

"Hey, Mari, is Rom here?"

"Yeah, he's in his room. Go on back."

Marisa sat back in a recliner as both of her little sisters made their way into the living room to join her. Nadia and Isi loved the novellas too, but they were really more interested at getting a look at Trent's new truck.

The three sisters looked a lot alike. Nadia looked most like Marisa, but she was heavier and shorter than her older sister and way more serious. She wanted to be a doctor. Whereas Isi, being the baby of the Maldonado family, was still very playful. She was only eight years old. She craved attention and knew how to get it.

When Trent finally knocked on the door, Isi beat Marisa to it. "Hey, Trent! Can I see your new truck? Will you take me for a ride? Please."

He gave her a wink. "Of course I'll take you for a ride. Nadia, you comin' too?"

"And what about me?" Marisa asked him. "Are you even going to say hello?"

"Hey, baby," he said, giving her a peck on the lips. "This is only for little sisters." She only gave him a little grief. She loved the fact that Trent treated her family like his own. In the months that they had dated, he had gotten close to her siblings and parents. It was as if he had always been a part of their lives. She couldn't have asked for anything more.

When they got to the truck, he rolled the top back. "Okay, ladies, let's roll out before me and Rom hit the strip." He pulled out and slowly drove down the street. Isi stood up excitedly. "Girl, sit down before you fall out of the truck," he told her. "Marisa would kill me."

"I'm not going to fall out," she retorted.

"Down, Isi," Nadia told her, "or we are heading back in."

"Okay, okay. Y'all know how to ruin a party."

When they got back home, Romero and Samuel were waiting. Romero's eyes lit up like a Christmas tree when he saw Trent's truck.

"Nice ride," he said.

"For real," Samuel agreed.

"Thanks for the ride, Trent. This is a beautiful truck," Nadia told him seriously.

"Anytime," he said to Nadia. "Bye, squirt," he told Isi. She kissed him on the cheek and ran in the house.

"Now let's get into some grown man stuff," Romero said, putting his black sunglasses on.

Trent drove through Port City like a man on a mission. Everyone was out, even though school started the following day. People blew their horns when they noticed it was Trent driving. He was used to all the attention, but Romero and Samuel were not.

"Does everybody know you?" Samuel asked, confused.

"Nah, nobody knows *me*. They know Trent Walker the basketball hopeful, but

Trent Walker the man, nah. When people see you have talent, they all want to be your friend, but they don't stop to get to know you. That's why I like Marisa so much. I feel like I finally met somebody who likes me for me and not my basketball skills," he responded.

When they pulled up at the seawall, it looked like the same people were out from the night before. Trent knew that he couldn't stay long; he wanted to get back to Marisa. They got in the long line of cars that made a mini parade along the coastline. It was a hot Texas day, but there was a cool breeze coming across the water. The girls weren't wearing much. Some wore bikini tops and shorts, others wore mini dresses or short skirts with skimpy tops. They wanted to be noticed. When they saw Trent, they always added a little extra twist in their step.

"Dude, if I could only be you for a day," Samuel said.

"Me too," Romero said.

As soon as Trent was about to park, he saw a few of the guys from the team. Ashton ran over to the truck. "Yo, dude, tell these fools that Michael Jordan had more skills in his time than Kobe and LeBron combined."

Trent laughed at his best friend. He always enjoyed Ashton's company. He was funny and genuine all at the same time. "Rom, y'all go peep the scene, and I'll text you when it's time to bounce."

It wasn't long before Romero and Samuel met up with some of the other eighth graders who went to Central Middle School. It was their year to rule the school. This group of kids wasn't Romero's usual crowd, but he'd had classes with them over the years. They were known for being the school misfits. Samuel went straight over to the leader of their crew and dapped him up.

"Young Sosa!" he called Sam as a play

on former pro baseball player Sammy Sosa's name. Romero found that odd. Samuel had played some baseball growing up, but he was definitely no Sammy Sosa.

"Big G!" Sam said. "This is Romero, my ace in the hole."

"Yeah? Any friend of Young Sosa is a friend of mine." It was easy to see that Big G was probably not supposed to be in the eighth grade. He seemed older and harder than the other kids in the circle. And he was much bigger—probably why they called him Big G.

The two boys stayed with the group for a while, just sitting on top of the cars and watching the girls walk by. They talked to a few of the kids that they knew from school. It was a great day for Seawall Sunday, and everyone was enjoying it.

"Cool. Hey, that's Trent textin'. We gotta be out. Let's go 'Young Sosa.'"

"Catch y'all at school tomorrow," Big G said.

"Yeah," the two boys said in unison as they went to meet Trent.

"How do you know him?" Romero asked Sam as they walked the seawall.

"Big G? He moved to my street at the end of last school year. We've hung out a couple of times. Why?"

"He doesn't seem like your normal crowd."

"Nah, he's harmless. People think he's bad. He says he's misunderstood."

"Yeah, well, I can see why," Romero said, unsure about Sam's choice of friends. By that time, they were at the truck.

"One more zip down the seawall and we're gonna head in," Trent announced.

"Sounds like a plan," Romero said, happy to be back with Trent where he was comfortable. He didn't like being around Big G and his friends. Frankly, he couldn't understand how Samuel could be either.

CHAPTER 2

Brandi

As Brandi stood looking at her reflection in the mirror, she couldn't believe the summer had gone by so fast. She was going back to school today. Her dramatic rescue seemed like yesterday. Everyone else was happy that she was back and life had resumed normally ... at least for them. For Brandi, nothing would ever be normal again. She was traumatized by her kidnapping.

As she looked at her reflection and imagined what her day was going to be like, she started to cry. The tears began to pour from her eyes, and she couldn't seem to stop them. She could hear her mother and Raven moving around the house, getting ready for the day, but she wasn't prepared to face them.

Thank goodness her dad was still in rehab in San Antonio. He was one less person she had to explain to why she didn't seem happy to be home. To everyone else, she seemed ungrateful. But that wasn't the case at all. She was extremely happy to be home and safe. But bad dreams plagued her at night, and the feeling that Steven was still somewhere out there watching her was terrifying. Maybe if he had been taken to jail and she knew where he was, she would feel better.

Mrs. Kennerson had seen to it that her son was not going to see the inside of a prison cell. The day Brandi was rescued, Mrs. Kennerson whisked him away before the cops had a chance to arrest him. Brandi's mom had pleaded with her to tell them where he was. The cops threatened to take her to jail, and still Mrs. Kennerson did not budge. Protecting Steven seemed to be her mission.

Sometimes Brandi wondered if Mrs. Kennerson thought about how she must feel knowing that Steven was still out there—or if she even cared.

The one thing Brandi thought would snap her back to normal was cheerleading camp, but she was so paranoid about him being somewhere close that she couldn't even enjoy it. The more she thought about what he had done to her—what he had taken away from her—the more depressed she became. She began to sob uncontrollably and curled back up in her bed. She could hear her mother calling her to come to breakfast, but she couldn't move. Then she heard footsteps on the stairs.

"Brandi?" she heard her mother say. Ugh. She wanted to be left alone. "Brandi, what's wrong, baby?"

"I can't do this, Mom," she said, sounding as though she was hyperventilating.

"Brandi, you have to calm down. Take a deep breath and talk to me. You can't do what?"

"I can't go back to school right now. Everyone will be looking at me and talking about me. It's too much. I can't go back, Mom. Please don't make me."

Mrs. Haywood's heart broke for her daughter, but she knew that the first day back would never be easy. She couldn't let her stay home or it would get harder and harder to go back. "Brandi, listen to me, baby. You have to go to school today. You need to get back to your regular routine and put this whole thing behind you."

"I don't even know if I was promoted to the next grade, Mom. It will be awful to be a freshman again while all of my friends are sophomores. Going back to school is easier said than done. I'm the one still having nightmares and looking over my shoulder. I'm scared all the time, Mom, and I don't know what to do," she cried as her mother held her.

"You're going to be fine, baby girl, just fine. I talked to your counselor already, and you are a sophomore. Once they saw how well you did on the state exams, they knew it would be crazy to hold you back a grade level," her mother said as she rocked her in her arms. "My smart girl. Now go wash your face and get ready for school. I'm taking you there myself. We will get through this together."

It made Brandi feel a little bit better knowing that her mother was going to bring her to school. If she felt uncomfortable, then she could come back home. She knew that her mom would understand. When she got downstairs, she looked like her old self again. Nobody would believe that she had just recovered from a breakdown only minutes before.

"Hey, B!" Raven said, excited to see her

sister. "You like the new hair bow Mama got me for the first day of school?"

"Of course. You look so cute, Ra-Ra," Brandi said, giving her a morning kiss. If it wasn't for Raven believing and convincing everybody else that she could help solve the mystery of Brandi's disappearance, she might still be trapped in that cabin with Steven. She lived for her little sister.

"Are you girls ready?" Mrs. Haywood asked, coming down the stairs.

"Sure, Mom, let's go," Brandi said, taking a deep breath. But when she got outside, Trent, Ashton, Shane, and Marisa were there sipping on cappuccinos and laughing loudly.

"Hey, what are you dorks doing here?" Brandi asked playfully, taking her drink from Shane's outstretched hand.

"Now I know you didn't think we were going to let you go back to school on the first day by yourself," Marisa said, giving her a hug.

Brandi had almost forgotten about her mom and sister. "Hey, Mom, I think I'm going to ride with them."

"Well, I figured as much," her mother said, smiling.

Brandi walked over to Raven. "Have a good day at school. Be careful. And don't talk to strangers," she warned her little sister with tear-filled eyes.

"You be careful too, B," Raven said.

"Thanks for everything, Mom."

"No problem, baby. That's what mothers are supposed to do. I'm sorry that I was so caught up in your dad's problems that yours fell through the cracks for a while. Mama's back now, and whatever you need, I got you."

Her mother was right. She had been on her own when her dad's addiction got really bad last year. It was one of the reasons that she fell for that creep on the Internet. She hugged her mother tightly and wiped a tear from her eye. She was so happy that their relationship was getting better and that her mom had talked her into going to school. She knew that she had more healing ahead of her, but she was determined to get better.

"Okay, roll out time!" Brandi exclaimed. "I'm ready," she added, reassuring herself. They all climbed into Trent's Hummer after saying their good-byes to Raven and Mrs. Haywood and headed off to a new year at Port City High.

CHAPTER 3

Shane

The newness of high school had worn off for the sophomore class. As far as the eye could see, there were mobs of freshmen trying frantically to find their way around the new school. *So happy that's not me*, Shane thought. She had already paid her dues. She was now a sophomore and loved the way it felt.

Shane was exhausted, though. Her sister, Robin, had just given birth to her nephew, Aiden, a couple of weeks before school started. He was possibly the whitest little black baby Shane had ever seen. It was love at first sight when she met her nephew. She didn't know that it was possible to fall in love so fast.

Aiden cried a lot throughout the night, making it difficult for any of the Fosters to sleep. Shane took one of the night shifts so that Robin could get some rest.

Mrs. Foster had warned Shane to let Robin get through the night on her own and to get some sleep for school. But when she heard Aiden crying, her immediate reaction was to get up and help her sister. She couldn't leave her on her own.

Robin never imagined that having a baby would be so hard. Sometimes, in the wee hours of morning when she was alone with Aiden, she thought about how many times her own mother had done the same thing with her. She wondered if her mother had someone to help her make it through. It gave her a new respect for her mother.

Shane loved it that this semester her

first class was journalism with her favorite teacher, Mrs. Monroe. When she walked into the classroom, Mrs. Monroe gave her a huge hug. "How was your summer, Shane?" she asked.

"It was great, Mrs. Monroe, which made it even harder to come back."

"Well, I'll admit that getting up early was rough for a few days, but I love being back. You'll be fine."

"I'm ready to dive into photography this year. I've been studying shots this summer and can't wait to put my new ideas to good use."

"That's great, Shane. I can't wait to see your new skills." Just when they finished catching up, the tardy bell rang. "Okay, class. I'm Mrs. Monroe. Everyone should be able to look around and see some familiar faces. This is an upper-level class for those people who are already familiar with journalism. You have been hand-picked to run the school newspaper and yearbook as your own little business this year. I know many of you have already worked together, but let's start out by introducing ourselves. You will be working together to make sure that our school newspaper and yearbook are the best that they can be. I'm going to start out by introducing you to the photo editor for this school year, Miss Shane Foster."

Shane was caught totally off guard. She was going to be responsible for not only taking pictures but making the final decisions on which images would be used for online and print. It would be her job to make sure that the photos told a story and the print supported it. It was a huge responsibility.

"Hey, everybody," she started. "I don't know what to say. This is the first I've heard about my new job, so bear with me. Um ... let me just say that it's going to be an honor to work with you all this year. I was already excited, and now I'm super-excited, and

I can't wait to get started. Thanks, Mrs. Monroe. I won't let you down," she said as she sat back down. The class gave her a small round of applause.

"Thanks, Shane," Mrs. Monroe said. "Another person that I want to introduce is your new editor-in-chief, Mr. Ryan Petry." Ryan was a fair-skinned, gangly twelfth grader with serious gray eyes who only talked when it was necessary. By the look on his face, Shane could tell that he had been caught off guard too. Ryan had been in charge of the junior section of the yearbook last year while Shane had been in charge the freshman section. It seemed that they should have known each other a little better, but they never moved beyond pleasantries.

With everything that Shane had going on last year, she was surprised she even remembered his name. She'd had her own problems to deal with during the first semester when she was addicted to

Adderall, the ADHD medicine, and then Brandi's abduction last spring really threw her for a loop. Plus, Ryan seemed to only talk when he had something to say, not like her usual guy friends who always had jokes.

Ryan stood up and addressed the class. "I look forward to working with you to make this the best year of news for Port City High. My motto is 'I will not be outworked.' Hopefully, we can create a staff that feels the same way. Thanks." The class clapped for Ryan, and a few of the girls seemed to fall in love immediately. Give a boy a title, and you're giving a girl a crush. It was typical.

After everyone introduced themselves and gave a little background about what strengths they had, Mrs. Monroe passed out a list of the positions that were still vacant for the school newspaper and yearbook. While everyone looked at the list of openings, Shane went over to introduce herself to Ryan. "Hey, I don't think that we've formally met," she said.

"Well, I'm Ryan. Ryan Petry."

"Shane, Shane Foster," she said, mimicking his introduction, but he didn't seem to find it funny.

"It looks like we'll be working together a lot this year. Did you know about her announcement?" he asked.

"Not at all. You?"

"No, but I'm excited," he said. "I plan to run a tight ship. You up for it?"

"I'm all about it," Shane said. "I can't wait to get started."

The bell rang as they finished their conversation. "Everyone, have a great first day," Mrs. Monroe said. "You are dismissed."

As lockers clanged shut, friends excitedly reconnected, and the sounds of high school surrounded Shane as she walked down the hall. Even though the end of summer had been sad, she was happy to be back and was ready for the new school year.

"This is going to be a great year. I can feel it," she said as she fell into the sea of students in search of their second period classes.

CHAPTER 4

First Lunch

The best part of this school year was that Shane, Marisa, and Brandi all had the same lunch schedule. It was their time, and they could spend it with each other. They met up at the cafeteria door before heading inside.

"Where are we going to sit this year?" Shane asked as she scoped out the scene in the lunchroom.

"Somewhere out of sight," Brandi said, noticing a table in the back.

"Now you know I like being by the door leading to the courtyard. Then we can see everybody. The lunchroom is just like life, the most important thing is your location, and that table is prime real estate."

"Not this year, Shane," Brandi said. She was annoyed at Shane for forgetting that she didn't want to be in the middle of everything.

"Ladies," Marisa said, moving through the crowd. "Follow me." She picked the perfect table. It was close to the crowd but off to the side, enough to give them some privacy. "Welcome home," she said as if she was opening the door to a brand new mansion.

"Perfect," Brandi and Shane agreed. They headed out to get lunch, but Marisa stayed behind to keep an eye on their table.

As she looked around the crowded lunchroom, she spotted Ashley Rivera coming her way. Marisa and Ashley had been at odds since their friendship had ended years ago. They were once very close, but Ashley's jealously over Marisa's friendship with Shane and Brandi had soiled their relationship. After numerous petty arguments, they had become hard-core enemies.

During the summer, Ashley had tried out for the twirling squad that Marisa was on, and she had made it. Seeing Ashley every day this summer for practice made their relationship even more testy. Usually, Marisa was able to ignore Ashley, but now she *had* to talk to her. It had been miserable for Marisa to have Ashley intruding into one of her favorite activities. She was sure that Shane and Brandi were sick of hearing her complain.

"Hey, Marisa!" Ashley said excitedly. Marisa knew that even when Ashley was being nice, there was probably something behind it.

"Hey," Marisa responded dryly.

"I think we should have a truce this year. I mean, with both of us on the twirling squad, it would be nice if we could just try to get along with one another."

She sounded so sincere. Marisa almost wanted to believe her. "All we can do is try, right, Ashley?"

"Yeah, well, I at least want to try. We've been through too much not to." As she was finishing up with Marisa, Brandi and Shane came around the corner with their lunches. "Hey, Brandi. What's up, Shane?" Ashley said.

"Hey," Brandi said cautiously.

"What's up with you?" Shane asked, eyeing Ashley as if she had been replaced by a clone.

"Look, I know this may sound crazy, but I really would like us to start over this year. I was just saying to Marisa that it is way too weird for us to be on the same twirling squad and not be able to coexist. I know to win her over I have to start with all three of you. So ..."

"Yeah, okay," Shane said, sounding skeptical.

"I'm good with this," Marisa said, sounding hopeful. "I think that it's a really good idea."

"Well, I'm from Missouri," Brandi interrupted. "The 'Show-Me State.' I've got to see this one to believe it." They all laughed.

"I'll do just that. Hey, better yet, we're having a block party Saturday night to celebrate our first victory. You all should come by my house. It's gonna be epic."

"We'll definitely think about it," Shane said.

"Cool, you know my girls are going to be there and some of the other twirlers. Bring some people if you like. We will have enough of everything for everybody. Laters," she said as she walked away.

"Odd, totally odd," Shane said, shaking her head.

"Oh, I think it's coming from a good place," Marisa said.

"Yeah, hell. Right where she came from," Brandi said, laughing.

"B!" Marisa said, slapping her arm.

"You know it's true," Brandi said. "That girl is trouble, and I don't trust her at all."

"Me neither," Shane added quickly. "She's always up to something."

"Well, I know I need to try to get along with her. I can't stand having beef on the squad. We are usually one big happy family, and I don't want to be the cause of us not being friendly."

Ashley had been the root of so much of the drama in their lives for nearly five years. Imagining her as a friend and ally was very difficult. Trust was something that had to be earned, and she hadn't earned any from them.

"What's that girl up to?" Shane asked, nodding her head toward Ashley.

"I don't know, but I'll bet money we'll find out soon," Brandi said.

"Y'all stop. I'm trying to be hopeful. Just try for me, okay?" Marisa asked them.

"All right, but watch your back. I'd hate to be the one who has to pull the knife out of it," Shane warned her.

CHAPTER 5

Marisa

The week of the truce between Marisa and Ashley had been surprisingly pleasant. Instead of avoiding her, Marisa had actually been talking to Ashley during warm-ups and helping her get ready for the first big football game. Ashley had not been on the squad last year. Practice and game night were very different. If you let your nerves get the best of you, the possibility of messing up became very great.

"I'm so nervous about getting on the field in front of all of those people," Ashley said.

"Don't be nervous. You're going to do fine," Marisa encouraged her.

"Hey, thanks for everything. I'm so happy we're friends again."

Hearing her say that they were friends again warmed Marisa's heart. She genuinely hated having beef with anyone. "Yeah, me too," she said, giving Ashley a huge hug. "Who would have thought?"

"I know, right?"

"Hey, you wanna come to Jerry's with me and Trent after practice?"

"I don't want to be a third wheel. Does he have any cute friends on the basketball team that he can hook me up with?"

"I thought you were dating Javier."

"Nah, that fool was texting some girl in Houston. You know I'm not down with that."

"I'll text Trent and tell him to bring somebody."

"Make sure he's a cutie!"

Marisa and Ashley finished up at

practice, showered, and headed to the gym to meet Trent. When they arrived, he was already outside with one of his teammates. Their hair was still wet from showering after practice, towels draped around their necks, and looking fit enough to make most females drool. Marisa's face lit up when she saw Trent. "Hey, baby," she said, giving him a kiss and a tight hug.

"Hi, I'm Ashley."

"Dalton Broussard," Trent's teammate said, flashing a smile that could make ice melt. Dalton was the power forward for the PCH basketball team. Girls were in love with Dalton. He had everything: the right clothing, the right kicks, the right family, the right house. They assumed that all he needed was the right girl, and then he would be complete.

"You two can get to know each other at Jerry's. I'm ready to eat," Trent said, walking toward his truck hand-in-hand with Marisa.

Ashley and Dalton got along great. By the time they finished eating, they had exchanged numbers and made plans to meet up at her upcoming party. When Marisa and Ashley escaped to the ladies' room, they could finally show their excitement. "Oh my ..."

"I *know*. Girl, I didn't know he was bringing Dalton Broussard. That's huge. It looks like you two are really hitting it off."

"I know, and he is so fine. I never thought I'd be going out with him. Seriously, I knew me and you were supposed to be friends for *some* reason. The stars aligned in our favor," Ashley said, looking in the mirror and touching up her makeup.

"The double dates are going to be insane."

"Wait until I tell the girls. They aren't too happy about the two of us hanging out," Ashley admitted.

"Yeah, well, Brandi and Shane aren't either."

"Really? I didn't get that from them," Ashley said sarcastically. They both laughed and headed out to meet their guys. It was getting late, so they decided it was time to call it a night.

Trent took Ashley and Dalton home first. He wanted to get some time alone with Marisa, which made her really happy. They sat in the truck and chatted now that they had complete privacy. Out of nowhere, Trent commented on Marisa's new friendship with Ashley. "So it looks like you and Ashley are getting pretty tight."

"Yeah, it's been kind of cool. I can't lie."

"Well, if you are cool with her, then she's cool with me."

Before they could get in a goodnight kiss, Mrs. Maldonado knocked on the door of the truck. "Mama, *qué pasa?*" Marisa asked, concerned.

"Mi hija, it's Romero. I haven't seen him tonight, and his phone is going straight to voicemail. Do you mind ..."

"No, ma'am, not at all. We'll pass by a few spots," Trent told her.

"Where can he be? You wanna go by Samuel's house first?" Marisa asked him.

"Yeah, I think that's a good place to start."

"I'm going to kill him for making Mom and Dad worry. He is going through such a rebellious stage. I don't even know what's up with that kid right now."

"Yeah, well, I went through it too at that age," Trent admitted. "Is that the house?" Trent asked, pulling onto Sam's street.

Sam lived in a neighborhood about five miles from where the Maldonado's lived. It was a neat neighborhood with small homes. Most of the families who lived there were made up of hard-working Hispanic parents who didn't make much but took good care of their families. Community was huge here. On any given Saturday night, a birthday party or celebration of some sort was under way. Although they were very close-knit, the youth seemed to be attracted to the street life. That's why the Maldonados preferred it when Sam came to visit their home and not vice versa.

"This is it. I'll go knock." Marisa went to the door and asked Mrs. Rodriguez if Sam and Romero were there, but she hadn't seen them. Mrs. Rodriguez had assumed that he was with the Maldonados. Now she was beginning to worry as well.

"What'd she say?" Trent asked, noticing the worried look on Marisa's face.

"She said that she hasn't seen them either. Now what?" Before she could complete her thought, they saw a group of kids walking toward them. "Let's ask if they know Rom and Sam. It can't hurt."

When Trent approached the teenagers in the Hummer, a guy in a black hoodie walked straight to the truck. It was dark, so they couldn't see his face until he got close. It was Romero.

"Qué pasa?" he asked, trying to see why they were there.

"Rom, your mother sent us out to find you," Trent said, sounding disappointed.

"Mama's been trying to call you, but it's going straight to voicemail. Just get in the truck. You have Mom and Dad worried sick. And, Samuel, you need to go home. Your mom is worried," she yelled, knowing that he was out there among the other boys.

"Quit trippin', Marisa," she heard Sam's voice say. The other boys laughed.

"Whatever. Don't act hard now," Marisa responded.

"Hey, Sam! I'ma catch you fools later," Romero said to his friend as he got in the truck.

"Who were those guys?" Marisa questioned. The smell of his clothing stopped her in her tracks. "Rom, I *know* you don't smell like weed."

"Aw, man, I do?" he asked.

"Have you been smoking, Rom? Don't lie to me."

"No, I haven't. You know I don't smoke. We were just hanging out at the bando down the street, and they were smoking. I was just chillin'."

Because of all the foreclosed homes in Port City, vacant houses were now a hotspot for teenagers. It was risky and dangerous now that law enforcement had gotten wind of it. Anybody caught in a bando, or abandoned house, could be brought up on charges, and the fines were said to be pretty hefty.

"Yeah, you chillin' now, but you lie with dogs, you bound to get fleas," Trent warned him.

"Trent, please give him some cologne. You know if you get caught in a bando, you are going to be in serious trouble, right?" Marisa said.

"Y'all too serious up in here. I was just chillin'."

"Well, Mama is not going to see it like that." They pulled up to the Maldonado house. Marisa was still fuming, but she had to help her brother diffuse the situation with her family. "Thanks for everything," she told Trent and jumped out of the truck. "Mama!" she yelled once she was in the house.

Her mother came running into the living room. "*Mi hijo*, where were you? I've been calling all over for you. You had me worried," her mother said, fussing over Romero like he was still five years old.

"He was with Samuel. I guess he didn't know that his phone had gone dead," Marisa said, covering for him. She couldn't leave him out there alone to get in trouble with her parents. She would have to deal with her brother at a later time. She had to find a way to reach him before he was too far gone.

"*Te amo*," he mouthed to Mari, telling her that he loved her. Her weak smile and narrowed eyes let him know that she was not amused by his antics. He left for his room, and she was left with her thoughts. She was disappointed in her brother tonight, but he was her heart. She had to look out for that kid.

CHAPTER 6

Shane

Friday night had finally arrived, and it was time for the first football game of the season between the Port City High Wildcats and the League City High Lions.

Before heading over to the game, Shane had a meeting in the photo lab to go over specifics with Ryan. She never had to meet with the editor-in-chief last year, so she was a little nervous about what this meeting was about.

Shane looked like the epitome of a photographer in her black skinny jeans and black tank top with her camera equipment in tow. Her hair was pulled up in a tight knot on top of her head. Her makeup was minimal except for the smoky eyes that went with her outfit. When she entered Ryan's office, he did a double take.

"You wanted to see me?" she asked.

"Yeah, I wanted to see your schedule for the photographers. There are certain shots I must have to make the articles work for this week's newspaper."

Shane handed the list that she e-mailed to her people. As he slowly read over it, she started to feel uneasy, like she should explain. "I feel that the schedule plays to everyone's strengths. If they know football better, I have them on the field. If they know—"

He cut her off. "It's fine. I think you did a great job. In the future, if you could send a copy of the schedule to me when you send it to everyone else, it will keep me in the loop."

"Okay, anything to help. It's your show."

"No, Shane, it's our show. From what I hear, this will be *your* office in your senior year."

"I haven't thought that far ahead," she said, contemplating the idea for the first time.

"Yeah, well, if I can do anything to help you, please let me know."

"I will. Thanks, Ryan. Well, I should get to work. I like to have some of my own pictures too. Guess I'm a little controlling that way."

"No, I like that. I'm the same way." There was an awkward silence that lingered.

"Well, I'll see you out there, I'm sure."

"Okay. Hey, Shane, do you have plans for after the game?" he asked, sounding more nervous than before. "I mean ... not like that. I wanted to go over the shots once the game is over."

"Oh, I can't. I'm going to the Room. They're throwing the football team a party tonight in their honor."

"Yeah, I heard about that. I've never been there before."

"Hey now, it's your senior year. You only live once. You should at least come."

"I just might do that," he said, opening the office door for Shane. You could see the stands from his office. The game was starting in thirty minutes, and the stadium was already packed. The buses were still unloading the rival band, cheerleaders, flag team, twirlers, and drum major, who anxiously awaited their grand entrance.

"I better get going. Looks like I'm missing some great shots," Shane told Ryan. She made her way down the path to the field. She was sure the Port City High band would give her classic photos she could use.

As soon as the band director gave the signal, the drumline began playing the beat to the fight song. Once the drums began, everyone came alive, and Shane documented all the moves through her lens.

In the crowded stands, fans could feel the base drum in their chests. The bleachers began to shake as the drum major flawlessly led the band. The flag girls and twirlers followed the band to the bleachers.

The first show took place right there in the stands as the catchy lyrics of Young Dub's song "BALLIN'... But I Don't Play" could be heard throughout the crowd. The students began to dance in their seats, under the bleachers, and at the concession stand, singing the chorus: *Ballin'... but I don't play ... Ballin'... but I don't play.* And posing in the signature Heisman Trophy stance that had become synonymous with Young Dub ever since the release of this top-selling single.

By kickoff, there were no seats left. Fans who arrived late were ushered to the end zone. Blue and silver-gray lawn chairs, embroidered with *PCH* over a wildcat paw print, lined the zone along with low-rise bleachers. It was a perfect night in Port City. Even though it was late August, the threat of a looming hurricane in the Gulf of Mexico created a mild breeze that cooled the crowd.

By halftime that breeze was needed because the Wildcats were down by one touchdown. The crowd was a little hot under the collar, but the Wildcats had been there before. The fans were sure that they would come back.

Shane headed to the field so she could get some shots of Marisa. She looked beautiful in her sequined leotard. Shane was able to catch the perfect shot of Marisa as she hit a beautiful windmill. Her face was flawless; her smile lit up the field. As Shane examined her shot, she knew that she had nailed it.

The Wildcats came back on the field, and, true to form, they took the lead. The home field advantage worked in their favor. They were a different team from the one on the field for the first half of the game. Their lead was so great that many of the fans started to leave at the beginning of the fourth quarter. They knew that it was a PCH victory, and they were ready to celebrate.

CHAPTER 7

Brandi

As the cheerleaders made it back to the parking lot and their rides, Brandi started to feel a little anxious in the big crowd. *What if Steven is here,* she thought. She knew that she had to get this guy out of her head, but it seemed to be getting harder and harder to put the ordeal behind her.

Now she had to get home to change, then put on a happy face and go to the Room with Shane and Marisa. She was thinking of opting out altogether as she stared out the car window.

"Turn that frown upside down. We

won the game," Christina said, sitting next to her friend. She knew that Brandi was still going through a lot. She wanted to be there for her, but sometimes she seemed to go to a place that no words could reach. "Hey, you okay?" she asked in a more serious tone.

"No. That's my honest answer. I'm not okay," Brandi said as one tear rolled down her face. It made her feel better to say it. Every time someone asked her how she was doing, she would just say fine. Things weren't fine, though. She knew she needed some help getting through this, but she didn't know where to turn.

"You know, when you were gone for those months, it was really hard on me," Christina said.

"No offense, Chris, but I think it was harder on me than you, ya know?"

"Yeah, of course. But it *was* hard. It was hard enough that I had to go to a support group for teens."

Brandi looked at her, shocked. "You did? What was that like?" she asked.

"It helped. For a while people were saying that you might not ever come back. My mom told me that I had to deal with that possibility, or it would destroy me. She found the group for me, and they were there for me when I needed them." Christina paused, watching Brandi as she processed what she had just been told. She sensed that Brandi was interested in going to the group. "I can go with you if you like," she said as she nudged her. She could see a small smile on Brandi's face.

"That would be nice," Brandi said. She took a deep breath. For the first time since she had been home, there was a glimmer of hope that she could get better; be well again. Maybe this group was exactly what she needed—a place where she could be honest.

"So, who are you going to the Room with tonight?" Christina asked.

"Marisa and Shane. We're staying at Shane's house. Are you going?"

"I've been thinking about it. You know I'm driving now, so I may go."

"I can't wait until I get to drive. That is so cool. I think I'd drive out of Port City if I could."

"And where would you go?"

"I don't know. Anywhere but here."

"You're crazy. Port City is it. I love this place. I will live and die in Port City."

"Not me. I'm leaving as soon as I can." Brandi's house was the first stop for the carpool. "Hey, Chris, thanks for everything. I feel a little better."

"Anytime, B. Hey, y'all want me to pick you up tonight?"

"Definitely. Meet us at Shane's. They'll be stoked. The girls love you."

About an hour later, Christina showed up at Shane's house. She loved the homes in this neighborhood. The house that

Christina grew up in was much smaller, but her mother had great taste and kept it beautifully decorated. She appreciated what she had but knew that one day she would fill a similar large home with her own family.

"Hey, Christina," Mrs. Foster said, opening the front door. "Come on in. The girls are upstairs."

"Yes, ma'am. I'll go hurry them along," she said with a smile. "Yo, yo, yo!" she said, pushing the door to Shane's bedroom open. Shane, Marisa, and Brandi were piled up in the restroom finishing their makeup and getting their look together.

"Hey, Christina," Brandi yelled. "Do you need to finish up too?"

"Nah, girl. I'm laid," she said. Her neat little bob went flying as she shook her head from side to side. Christina's beautician had hooked her up and talked her into adding bangs this time to frame her face. She looked like a little brown doll.

Her skin was the most beautiful shade of brown, similar to a caffé latte from Starbucks. She was like a person on Vivarin—always up—always down for whatever. "Let's roll out. I want to see who's getting their swag right this year."

Shane liked hanging out with Christina. They didn't do it much, but when they did, she seemed like an older version of herself. "Hey, I'm down. I look at my boys like library books. I check out a cutie and turn him in before the due date," she said, laughing.

"And how do you know when they're due?" Christina asked.

"When they start getting on my nerves," she said.

"Okay," Christina said, dapping Shane up. They piled into Christina's white Mustang convertible. She'd gotten it when her mom got an SUV. "Okay, we have to flip the strip before we go to the Room," she told the girls.

"We're right there with you," Shane told her. She was riding shotgun. "Drop the top and let's see what's hot. I want to hear something good, and I'm tired of Young Dub, so don't even say it."

"I have something for you. This is the best female artist in Texas."

"Who is this? I love that beat," Brandi said, dancing in her seat.

"Lil Flo, she's from the four-oh-nine," Christina said as she started to rap along with the music. "She just signed with Third Coast Records."

"She's my new favorite. I'm all over this," Shane said as they pulled up at the Room.

"Girl, me too. I'm going to be *the* female Hispanic artist from Texas," Marisa laughed.

"Don't quit modeling. I heard you free-style before, and it's not what's up," Brandi said, making fun of Marisa.

CHAPTER 8

Party-Packed Weekend

As they walked into the Room, they felt the same familiar vibe. As usual, the guys lined the walls trying to look hard while checking out females. The girls walked around in the skimpiest outfits trying to get chosen. There was a mating game going on that everyone pretended didn't exist, but it filled the room like air fills a balloon. You couldn't see it, but you knew it was there.

When Marisa saw Trent, her heart skipped a beat. Ashley had already made her way over to him. They were laughing heartily at something. "Hey, my peoples," Marisa said.

"Baby girl," Trent said, catching her up in a huge hug. He kissed her neck, and she melted in his embrace. She was happy she wasn't out there looking thirsty like those other girls. She had her man, and he was all hers.

"Hey, Ashley, where's Dalton?" Marisa asked, looking for the other part of their little group.

"I don't know. He was right here, but when I came over, he seemed to magically disappear."

"Aw, it's all good. Hey, want to take a quick stroll with us. We're just getting here." Brandi and Shane had fallen to the side with Christina and were talking to Trent and Ashton while they waited for Marisa to finish up with Ashley.

"No, I think I'll just chill," Ashley said, glancing over at Brandi and Shane, who didn't look really enthused about having her tag along. "My girls are waiting for me anyway. I just came over to holler at Dalton and wound up talking to Trent. Hit me later."

As she walked away, Ashley looked a little down over Dalton's obvious diss. Marisa felt sorry for her, but she didn't want to get caught up in their drama when she was all good with Trent. She could feel Brandi and Shane staring her down. "Be careful of that one," Shane warned her.

"Y'all need to cut Ashley some slack," Trent said. "I think she's coming from a good place."

"That girl's a ticking time bomb," Brandi told them. "She's as good as she is evil."

"Okay, let's get our dance on. I'm going to see if the DJ has that new Lil Flo we were jammin' to in the car," Shane said.

Shane sashayed her way up to the DJ booth and wound up on the mic giving shout-outs and getting the crowd hyped. She introduced Lil Flo like she knew her personally. DJ Dazed slipped her his card when she was done. He was a cutie with a neat little Mohawk, cut to perfection. He wore a neon-colored polo, sagging Levi's, and the hottest neon Nikes. He was Shane's type, a pretty boy with swag who had a job.

She jumped off the stage and went to find her girls, but she ran into Ryan Petry on the way. He was the opposite of DJ Dazed, clean-cut, serious, but obviously interested in Shane too. She could tell because he seemed nervous when she was around. She found it both dorky and cute.

"Ryan, hey. I didn't think you'd show," she said flirtatiously. She was in her zone and ready to play a bit.

"That was a pretty impressive show you put on up there. So you're a photographer and a hype man ... I mean woman."

Shane laughed. "Yeah, you could say I'm a Jackie-of-all-trades. I love a micro-phone and a camera."

"You should be in front of the camera," he said, looking as if he immediately regretted it. He started to blush. Shane loved the effect she had on him.

"Hey, come dance with me," she told him, wanting to be active instead of just talking.

"I don't really dance," he said.

"It's okay. Let's let loose." She figured out why he didn't dance. He couldn't. The boy had two left feet. She danced with him for a couple of songs and then found a way to get away from him without being obvious. He was fun to flirt with here and there, but that was it. He was an important person in her journalism world. And she liked being connected to his level of power.

When she met back up with Christina, Brandi, and Marisa, they were in their element, surrounded by the basketball team. Ashton had just pulled yet another prank on Brandi, and she chased him through the group but never caught him. Even from far away, anyone could tell they were having fun. If you weren't a part of this group, you wanted to be. They were enjoying themselves and oblivious to the effect they had on other people.

Trent was leaning on the wall, and Marisa was dancing with Christina and Brandi. Shane joined her girls while Ashton and Dalton both looked her up and down. "What?" she asked. "Why y'all looking at me like that?"

"I was telling Dalton how ugly you looked tonight, and he was agreeing," Ashton told her playfully.

"Yeah, back at you, bro," she said, punching him hard in the arm.

"Shane, that hurt," Ashton said. "I told you she was ugly."

"Nah, not to me," Dalton said, looking at Shane seriously.

"You need to stop, Dalton. I know you and Ashley have a thing going. I don't want any parts of that."

"We went out on one date. It was cool. Don't get me wrong, but you are way more my style," he said, grabbing her by the hand.

Ashley could see everything that was taking place, and Dalton was breaking her heart right there in front of everybody. She had told all of her friends how much they had hit it off, and now he was over there flirting with Shane. Ashley was so embarrassed. She ran to the bathroom before she could see Shane shoot him down.

"Look, Ashley and I are not friends by any means, but I don't dip down that low. Sloppy seconds ain't my style," she said, taking her hand back from Dalton.

"I knew you didn't have a chance. I told you. You can't have them all, D," Ashton joked, laughing.

"Yeah, well, I still got your mama's

number, so I'm good," Dalton told him. Everyone in earshot began laughing, and Ashton chased Dalton as the lights flickered on and off, indicating that the party was coming to a close.

Dalton rounded the corner and ran into Ashley, who was coming out of the restroom. "Hey," he said. "Am I still going to see you tomorrow?"

"Do you want to see me tomorrow?" she asked, confused. "It looked like you wanted to see Shane instead."

"What? You buggin'. Is that why you kept your distance from me tonight?" he asked.

"I was trying to spend time with you, Dalton ... whatever," she said, rolling her eyes.

He grabbed her hand, pulled her close, and kissed her in the middle of the dance floor.

"Ooh, kissies," Brandi said to Shane. Shane laughed, knowing that Dalton was trying to get Ashley's attention again after she had rejected him.

"Dalton Broussard has issues and so does Ashley. This should make for an interesting school year."

The party at Ashley's house was on Saturday. You would have thought that summer hadn't ended yet if you didn't know any better. The first weekend after school started, there were five parties happening in Port City. The beginning of the school year basically set the tone for the whole year. Everybody was trying to get "chose." The perfect boyfriend/girlfriend duos were blossoming and love was in the air in Port City.

At Ashley's block party, the DJ was spinning old school hip-hop and new school rap, and he had the whole street rocking. She lived in a nice mixed community that was similar to Brandi, Shane, and Marisa's neighborhood. The neighbors didn't mind that a huge block party was going on right in front of their houses. The people who had teenagers opened their doors for partygoers to be able to get food and drinks. There seemed to be a cool vibe.

Brandi, Shane, and Marisa went straight to the Rivera house. Marisa wanted to let Ashley know they were there. When they arrived, she could tell that the attitude toward her had changed. Ashley and her friends had been drinking, so their mood was strange. "What's up, Ma-ri-sa? This is my new BFF, y'all!" Ashley was saying loudly while slurring her words.

"You okay?" Marisa asked her.

"Yeah, I'm fine. It's you who tripped out. I thought it was all cool between us. Then you tried to hook Dalton up with Shane. He told me all about it."

"You're drunk, Ashley, but that's no excuse for being stupid," Marisa said, turning to leave. "Everybody warned me not to trust you. I'm such a fool. Stay out of my life."

"Good riddance!" Ashley yelled.

"Just FYI, Ash-ley," Shane said. "Dalton did try to holler at me, and Marisa had nothing to do with it. So whatever he told you was a lie. You broke her heart over a lie. Wait up, Mari!" Shane yelled.

Brandi joined Shane as they caught up to Marisa. "I don't want to hear 'I told you so,' so save it."

"We're not going to say we told you so. Just wait," Brandi said.

Marisa was in tears. She turned around to face her friends for the first time.

"Don't you dare cry over her," Shane said sternly.

"I thought she had changed. I feel so stupid," Marisa said. "Get me out of here."

Luckily, they didn't have to go far to find a ride. Christina was pulling up to the party, and they jumped in the car with her.

"Please get us out of here," Brandi said to her through the window.

They cruised the strip to clear their minds and headed to the football party going on at the pier. It was packed—hopping much more than Ashley's party. It was a great transition from how the night had started out. The vibe at Ashley's was sour with all of the drinking; they felt it as soon as they got there. But at the pier, fun was tangible, and they were enjoying every minute.

CHAPTER 9

Marisa

The newness of the beginning of school wore off quickly. Fun and parties had been replaced by homework and practices. For Marisa, the biggest downside was the awkwardness between her and Ashley.

It was different when they were enemies. The little time that they had spent together as friends made things even tenser, and everyone else could feel it too. The whole twirling squad felt like they were being forced to choose sides, and that was the last thing Marisa wanted. Trent tried to talk to her about reaching out to Ashley, but there was no way she was ready for that yet.

As summer seemed to melt away, the leaves turned from green to the brilliant colors of orange, red, and yellow. Fall had officially arrived, and the Wildcat football team was still undefeated.

Spirits at PCH were high, and the twirlers were practicing like never before. The routine that they were set to perform pushed them to the limit. Each twirler would have a solo on the field this week.

To build momentum with the music, the level of difficulty increased down the line. Marisa wanted to nail a baton toss and triple turn that would put her next to last in the line, which was right in front of the captain. She practiced and practiced and finally got it perfectly. As she tried to perform the trick in front of the other twirlers, something happened. Her feet didn't do what her head told them to do. Her left leg wrapped around her right leg and sent her falling to the ground. The other twirlers rushed to her side as she screamed out in agony.

"Don't move her," she heard her captain say.

Ashley was the one by her side, holding her hand through the whole ordeal. Two of the twirlers took her to the emergency care facility for the athletes that they had on campus. Again, Ashley was close by. When the other twirlers sat down to wait on the nurse to come in, Ashley told them she would stay with Marisa. The nurse took forever to get there, and Marisa was in so much pain. Tears ran down her face, and she grimaced from the discomfort.

"I'll go find some ice to put on your ankle," Ashley said to her.

"Please, I'll take anything at this point," Marisa told her.

Marisa's right ankle was really beginning to swell. When Ashley returned, she gently laid some icepacks across Marisa's leg, which was beginning to turn black and blue.

"Wow! Those icepacks are really helping," she said. "Where did you find all this?"

"I snuck into the therapy room for the athletes. They have everything in there. I could wrap it too, but I'll leave that to the professionals. Marisa, I know this isn't the right time, but I thought I should apologize for what happened at my party. I was really hurt. I thought Dalton was into me, and when I saw him with Shane—"

"No worries, Ashley. Thanks for apologizing."

Finally, the nurse came rushing through the door. Ashley stepped into the hallway to give Marisa time alone with her. "I'm so sorry. I got held up. One of the guys on the track team took a pretty nasty fall too. Let's see how you're doing." She raised the icepacks gently off of Marisa's ankle, making her wince. The nurse examined it. "It's probably a bad sprain," she explained, "but you'll need an X-ray to be sure. Regardless, you'll have to stay off your ankle for at least two weeks."

"I cannot take two weeks off. Football season isn't long enough to sit out for two games. I'll die," she said as tears filled her eyes.

"Marisa, you really won't die," the nurse said as she wrapped her ankle. "Everything will be fine. I bet you'll be all better by homecoming."

That cheered Marisa up a bit. At least she wouldn't have to miss homecoming. It was the highlight of the fall.

"Just elevate your ankle and use this icepack for the initial swelling. You'll be okay. I'll get your friend back in here to help you out. And don't forget about that X-ray."

When the nurse opened the door, Marisa could see straight into the hallway. Trent had shown up to check on her. He was standing with Ashley, who had a huge smile on her face. She threw her long hair flirtatiously as she looked up at Trent, unaware that she was being watched.

"Hey, baby," Trent said nervously. "Ashley sent me a text and told me to meet y'all over here." When he entered the small room, it seemed to shrink.

"How does she have your number to text you?" Marisa asked suspiciously. She didn't want to seem ungrateful, but something wasn't right.

Ashley spoke up right away. "I got his number from Dalton. It's really no big deal. I thought that I was doing you a favor."

"You were. I know," Marisa said, feeling like she'd overreacted. "Hey, no worries. I'm sorry I said anything. You've been super-supportive today. I really appreciate it. Let's get home. I'm exhausted."

Marisa was quiet for most of the ride home. Her gut was still telling her that something was wrong. After they dropped

Ashley off and she was alone with Trent, she finally felt comfortable enough to speak. "What were you two talking about in the hall when I was seeing the nurse?" she asked.

"Marisa, come on now. You can't be so suspicious. She was saying that Dalton wasn't checking for her like she wanted. I tried to tell her that he was, but she was ready to give up on him."

"That's it? That's all she said? And she wasn't flirting with you?"

"I don't know. I mean, no. Shoot, Mari. Girls flirt with me all the time. After a while, you start to ignore it. When you are in love, that's what you do."

"In love? Are you trying to butter me up, Trent Walker? 'Cause it's working," she said, leaning over to give him a kiss.

Trent playfully carried Marisa into her house and over the threshold. She repeatedly told him that she could walk, but he would hear none of it.

"Mi hija, what happened?" her mother asked, concerned when she saw her daughter being carried into the house.

"I sprained my ankle. I have to stay off of it for two weeks, so no twirling for me. I'm bummed, but I'll be okay. Oh, and I'm supposed to get it x-rayed to be sure it's not broken."

"Well, as long as you are okay," her mother said, retreating to the kitchen to finish cooking dinner.

"Yo, Trent," Romero said, dapping him up. His eyes were half shut, and he was giggling and staring at Trent.

"Hey, Romero," Trent said, looking at Marisa a little confused as he returned the dap. He put Marisa down on the couch.

"Romero, are you high?" she whispered, pulling him close to her.

"Nah, I don't smoke weed. I did try some of that legal, though, but it's no big deal. They sell it now in the corner store. How bad can it be?"

"You are crashing, dude," Trent said, sounding disappointed. "Yo, Mari. I'm out. I'll let you handle this one," he said, bending down to kiss her.

Marisa was embarrassed—and furious with her brother. It had been such a long day. "Okay, I'll see you tomorrow," she said. As soon as Trent left the house, she turned angrily to Romero. "Dude, you are going in the wrong direction, for real."

"Nah, I'm doing me. You're mad that I'm making my own way now. Let me do me the way I want."

"Rom, come on. This isn't you. This sounds like those stupid gangbangers that you've been hanging with."

"Hey, they are not stupid. Gabino is chill, and he makes sure his crew is taken care of. They are like family, and I like that."

"You have a family already, Romero. We are your family. Your *real* family," she said, hopping up from the couch. Putting too much pressure on her swollen ankle

made her wince in pain, but she didn't
back down. "You sound like a gangbanger,
and you look like one too with your little
slanted eyes. I don't even recognize you,"
she said, getting angrier by the second.

"I am not a gangbanger."

"Not yet, but you will be if you keep it
up," she said, getting closer to her brother.

"Get out of my face, Mari. You in my
space."

"What you going to do, Romero? Big,
bad gangbanger," she said, slapping him in
the head.

"Man, I ain't gotta take this from you.
I'm out," he said and walked out the front
door. Marisa hopped after him, but she
was hurting too much to catch him.

By eleven, Romero still had not come
home. Marisa's parents questioned her
relentlessly about where he was. "He's only
thirteen, Marisa. He can't be out there
alone."

"He's not alone," Marisa said under her

breath. "Sometimes, you have to let people learn for themselves."

"What happened between the two of you tonight?" her father asked. She insisted that it wasn't important. Marisa couldn't believe how she'd gotten in her brother's face. She was willing to go toe-to-toe with him if it meant that she could stop him from going down the wrong path, but she couldn't save him from life.

When Romero stormed out of the house, he walked straight to the bando—where he'd been earlier that evening. Luckily, Big G had chosen an abandoned house closer to the Maldonados', so it only took him about twenty minutes to get there. He walked into the bando like he had never left to go home.

"Lil Rom, what you doing back here?" Gabino asked him.

"Man, I couldn't breathe at home. I had to get out of there. My family is a trip."

"Yeah, I don't know much about that. My mom left a long time ago, and my dad works out of town a lot, so most of the time it's just me. I consider my boys my family. You wanna hit some of this legal again?" he asked, extending a cigarette filled with a substance called Serenity.

"Why not? It is legal, right?" he asked.

"Would we call it legal if it wasn't?" Gabino laughed.

Everyone in Gabino's gang was at the bando that night. Even a few young hopefuls who wanted to be down had joined them. The girls had all been chosen and divided up amongst their crew. Romero felt like he was part of a secret society. He was on top of the world.

The only thing missing was Samuel. He sent him a text, but Samuel couldn't come. When he started getting tired, he wanted to go home, but he knew that it wasn't a good idea. There would be too much drama. He would have to sneak back in the morning when his sisters were at school. His mom would be there alone, and he could explain everything to her then.

A couple of the guys from the crew were going over to Jack in the Box and asked Romero if he wanted to get some food. "Nah, I'm good. I don't have any money with me," he said.

Gabino stepped in when he heard that. "Lil Rom, don't worry about money. We got you, *hermano*. That's how we roll."

"Thanks, Big G," Romero said, relieved that he could get rid of some of the hunger he was feeling.

As soon as they opened the door to head out for late night snacks, two police officers were walking up the front porch. They retreated back into the house yelling, "Five-oh, five-oh." Everyone inside scattered. It was a wild frenzy of people trying to gather the few belongings that they brought with them.

The police were yelling at them, "Freeze! Everybody stay right where you are." Their words only added to the chaos.

It took Romero a while to realize what was going on, and he was slow to react. He tried to run out of the house with a couple other guys, but he hadn't moved quickly enough. The larger officer grabbed him by the back of his hoodie. Before he knew it, he was being read his rights and questioned. He was so nervous that he didn't say anything. He didn't know what to say.

"How did you get into the house? What does all of this writing mean on the wall? Where did you get the synthetic weed from?"

Romero really didn't know the answer to any of their questions. He was just there; he wasn't really a part of the whole thing. He was read his rights, cuffed, and transported.

When they arrived at the police station, four of the other guys from the bando were already there. Including Gabino. Romero was surprised that they were able to catch him. He was the quickest and smartest of them all, but there he was, waiting to be processed. The whole thing was like one huge nightmare, and he was ready to wake up.

Romero had his head down when Gabino went to talk to him. "Say, Lil Rom, let me holla at you for a sec," he said.

Romero looked up at Gabino. He was trying to stay strong, but on the inside he was crying. He hadn't been allowed to call his parents. Nobody even knew where he was.

"What's up, Big G?" he asked.

"Dog, I want to make sure that you are cool. Did you tell those laws anything when they questioned you?"

"Nah, I just gave them a bunch of 'I don't knows,' so they put me in the back of the car and brought me here."

"Well, good. Let me go talk to these

other fools and make sure they don't have us catching a case."

"A'ight," Romero said and put his head back down. It seemed like he sat in the station holding area for days listening for his name. Waiting was the hardest part. Plus he was starving. He never did get that Jack in the Box he was offered. His mind raced as he sat there. There was nothing else to do but to think. *I wonder what my family's doing. Are they looking for me? Marisa's probably really mad. I really screwed up this time*, he thought.

"Maldonado, Romero Maldonado," he heard an officer say his name.

"Yeah, that's me," he said nervously, standing up as the eyes of his companions followed his every move.

Romero was led into a room to get his mug shot taken. He'd always wondered why people's mug shots came out looking so tired and sad, and now he knew why. He felt how they all looked.

Next he was fingerprinted and interviewed about any tattoos, piercings, or scars he had. Then, before they took him to a cell, he was strip-searched.

It was the most embarrassing thing he had ever been through in his life. *How did I get here?* he wondered. They made him take everything off, even his underwear. *This has to be the worst day of my life*, he thought.

After what seemed like an eternity, he was finally allowed to call his parents. He stated his name for the recording to let his family know who was calling collect from jail. He didn't want to hurt them, but he knew going to jail would do that.

When he heard his mother's voice, he started to cry. He told her as little as he could. Everybody warned him that the police were probably listening to his calls. Before she hung up the phone, she promised she would be there to pick him up, and she was. Even though she arrived at the jail within ten minutes, it still took two more hours before he was released. He was given a court date and sent home—back to his normal life. Thirteen years old and already in trouble with the law, he knew that something had to change.

As he stared out the car window on the ride home, he thought about Marisa and her words before he had walked out the door. She had been right all along.

CHAPTER 10

Shane

Shane!" Robin yelled from her room.

"What?!" she hollered back, walking into her sister's room.

"Don't you hear your nephew crying? Can you please come here and help me?"

"Robin, I'm editing some photos right now. I'll give you a break later. Just let me finish up."

"Shane, you always say that, and then you find some other excuse. I need help, and I need help now." The tears that welled up in Robin's eyes slowly began to trickle down her face. Shane's heart ached for her sister. Being pregnant had been rough. Aiden was going on three months now, and her sister still hadn't gotten back to her old self yet.

Shane had been curious about what to expect when her sister returned home from the hospital, so she gathered some information on the Internet. When she researched postpartum depression, she was convinced that her sister was suffering from PPD, as it was called. When she mentioned it to Robin, she was livid.

"Just because I've cried a couple of times, you think I'm depressed. I am not depressed. I need a little help sometimes, and I don't ever get any."

"I help you all the time," Shane rebutted. It was true. Shane did help her sister, but she had no idea all the things that were on Robin's plate when she wasn't around. Being a mother was a full-time job. Not getting any breaks was driving Robin crazy.

"Hey, give me Aiden," she said to her sister. "I'll edit the pictures another time. After all, it is Saturday, and I need a break too. Why don't you get out of the house for a while? Call Gavin. You two deserve to do something fun."

"Girl, you don't have to tell me twice," her sister responded. Robin threw on her snow boots over her Juicy Couture sweats, brushed her curly hair into a tight pony tail, brushed her teeth, and was out the door within ten minutes.

"Well, I guess it's just us," Shane said, smiling down at her nephew. Normally, he was in a great mood, but his face started to scrunch up like when he was about to cry. "What? What's the matter, little man?" she asked. By this time, he was in a full-blown scream. She tried to make a bottle for him, but he wouldn't take it. She tried to burp him, but that didn't work either. *Maybe he's wet*, she thought. When changing his diaper didn't help, she knew that she was in trouble. She tried calling her sister, but she heard Robin's phone ringing in her bedroom. Shane really didn't know what to do now.

Then she heard the garage door go up. Her mother must be home. A couple minutes later there was knocking on the bedroom door. "Robin," she heard her mother say. "What's going on in there?"

"No, it's me, Mom," she said, still trying to calm Aiden down.

"What are you doing?" her mother asked as she opened the bedroom door.

"I'm babysitting for Robin, but I can't get Aiden to stop crying. I've tried everything."

"Well, your sister needs to be here with him so you can focus on school. She graduated already. This is your time."

"I know, Mom, but somebody has to help her."

"Nobody helped me. She needs to be independent. She has a roof over her head and free food in her belly. Your sister will be okay. Give me Aiden." She pressed on his stomach, then she moved his legs around in a circular motion. "It seems like he's gassy." She gave him some drops of gripe water. Within two minutes, he stopped crying.

Shane knew there was no reasoning with her mom when it came to her sister's situation.

When her mother got pregnant, she wasn't speaking to her own mother, Shane's grandmother, and she was on her own. In her head, she thought that made it okay to not be there for Robin. But it wasn't okay, and Shane knew it. Sometimes she thought her mother was missing a sensitivity chip or something.

Grandma really messed her up, Shane thought. She adored her mother, but it was moments like these that made her adamant about not being like her.

When five o'clock rolled around, Shane

started to wonder if her sister was coming back home. She called Gavin to see when they were going to be back. "Hey, G," she said when he answered the phone.

"Hey, Shane, doggy dog. What's up?"

"Looking for sissy. Is she still with you?"

"No, I haven't seen her today. I've been at work."

"Oh," Shane said, surprised. "I don't know where she could be. Can I ask you something?"

"You just did."

"Ha-ha-ha, no for reals. Is Robin okay? She seems like she's struggling."

"I don't know, Shane," he said, taking a deep breath. "She's been pretty distant with me too." At that moment, Aiden woke up. He started to cry. "You have Aiden?" he asked.

"Yeah, I do. I told her to go spend some time with you, but I didn't know you were working Saturdays too."

"I have two jobs now. Every time I turn around, I have to buy something else for him. I have to have money coming in. It sucks that I can't really help your sister more with the baby because I'm always working."

"Well, I'm doing what I can, but you have to too. We are all that she has right now."

"I know, and thanks for being there for all of us."

"No worries. Hey, I'll talk to you later." She hung up the phone and threw on a movie while she waited for her sister to show up. "Guess I'm in for the long haul, little man," she said to Aiden as he looked up at his aunt.

CHAPTER 11

Brandi

*I*t was Brandi's second time coming to this group session at Helping Hands. The first time, Christina had gone with her and introduced her to a few of the people that she knew. Because she had shared so much about her own fears of Brandi's abduction, the group felt like they knew her too.

Brandi wasn't ready to talk during that first meeting. When she got home and thought about it, she knew she had to open up. Everyone else was very candid about what they had been through. She knew that if she was going to get better, she would have to open up too. And so she did.

"Hi, everyone, my name is Brandi Haywood. Some of you may know me as the girl who was on the missing child posters last school year. There are a lot of rumors out there about what happened to me during those two months. I'll give you the quick version. When I was eight years old, one of my best friends drowned in the lake. Her brother was the only person with her at the time. He wasn't able to save her life, and he basically lost it.

"He was released from a psychiatric hospital last year, and in some way, he thought having me was like having a piece of his sister back. At first, I didn't know who he was. I hadn't seen him since I was eight ..." She took a deep breath.

"When I figured it out, I was shocked, confused, and frightened. I felt like he wouldn't hurt me, but he had already roughed me up a couple of times, so I was cautious. If it hadn't been for my little sister and friends believing that I was alive, I might not be. Steven and I may have died together at that lake ..." She took another deep breath. "That's why I'm here. He's still out there, and I'm afraid he'll come back to finish what he started."

Everyone clapped for Brandi when she was done. The counselor in charge of the group was a round little lady with a sweet voice. She had naturally red hair and green eyes. She seemed like the perfect elementary school teacher. Everyone called her Ms. P because her last name was so difficult to pronounce.

"You are a very brave girl and even braver for sharing your story with us. Talking to others about what you've been through and are still coping with can be a powerful healing tool. Let's take a quick break. That was a lot to digest for a group of people that talked about you the entire time you were gone. We're so happy that you are home and safe," Ms. P said. The other students nodded in approval.

As they headed to the refreshment table, one boy approached Brandi as she was putting a slice of cake on her plate. "I wouldn't eat that if I were you," he cautioned. He was an attractive guy with beautiful long eyelashes and curly hair. Brandi noticed him when she was speaking to the group, but she wasn't here for romance. She wanted to heal here.

"And why not?" she asked him.

"Because it's dinner time and you probably haven't eaten a thing."

"True, that's why I'm having the cake."

"Hey, why don't you grab a burger with me instead?"

"I don't think that would be a good idea, Bryce," she said, reading from his name tag.

He smiled at her. "Look, you have to eat and I'm treating. I want to get to know you, and not the Brandi from the poster. I promise to take care of you. I know you've been through a lot, but you can let your guard down a little. That's part of the process too."

He said all the right things, and she began to soften. "Okay, but I have to be home early. I have homework."

When they left Helping Hands, they went to the burger shop on the corner to grab a bite to eat. Bryce swore that it was better than Jerry's, but the proof would be in the first bite.

"Oh my ... this is delicious," Brandi said quickly, wiping the secret sauce from her mouth. "Why have I never been here before?"

"Not too many people know about this spot. I come here with my mom whenever she gets clean and wants to hang out. That's how I found Helping Hands. They were all here one night, and I was ear hustling. They sounded like they had something that was working, and I wanted to be a part of it."

"That's why you go to Helping Hands? Your mom's an addict?" she asked, playing with a french fry on her plate.

"Yeah, it used to be hard on me, but now I know it really has nothing to do with me."

Brandi started to cry. She couldn't look at him. "I guess I'm here for that too. My dad's an addict," she said, admitting something that she tried to keep hidden from the world.

"Oh, wow, I didn't know. I'm sorry."

"Yeah, he's in rehab now."

"Have you gone to visit him yet?"

"No, I'm not going there."

"You should. It's nice to see who they are sober sometimes. You don't know how long it will last when he gets out. My mom's been to rehab three times already."

Brandi got lost in the thought that her dad would start using again. She assumed that this was the end of the road for his addiction, but now she wondered. "Hey, I need to be getting home," she said, sending a text to her mom.

"I shouldn't have said that. I'm sorry."

"No, you were honest. Thank you. I shouldn't be too hopeful, I guess."

"Do you mind if I change the subject?" he asked, grabbing her hand. "I know we just met, but I really want to know more about you. I want to spend time with you. Is that crazy?"

"Not at all," she said. Everything in her said that it was too soon to start dating again after being fooled by Steven. They made small talk until she saw her mom's car pull up. "Hey, that's my ride. Are you going to be okay?"

"Yeah, I'm good."

When Brandi got in the car with her mother, she was determined. "Mom, I need to go see Dad," she announced.

"But I thought—"

"I know what I said, but I need this. Raven needs to see Dad too."

"I do too," her mom said, looking vulnerable for the first time. "Well, there's no time like the present. San Antonio, here we come. We'll leave in the morning."

CHAPTER 12

Wildcat Homecoming

Homecoming week was insane. There was crazy hat day, teacher for the day, crazy socks day, and crazy hair day. The senior class was determined to do something different. They organized a huge carnival the Thursday night before the game. The whole school seemed to be in attendance. The football team set up a dunking booth and an old-fashioned kissing booth. It drove the little freshmen girls crazy, kissing the cheeks of seniors who they had a crush on.

"I can't believe they pulled off getting a carnival, with rides and everything, right here at school. This is so cool," Marisa said. She was in great spirits. The doctor had released her the day before, and her ankle had healed completely.

"We have to come up with something even better our senior year," Shane said. "We can't let their little class outdo us."

"Well, I'm enjoying what we have right here. I'm getting used to being in large crowds again. The support group I'm going to is really helping a lot," Brandi told the girls.

"Good, B. I'm glad to see you back to your old self again," Marisa told her.

The carnival had started during their last class. What was normally a soccer field was now a full-on carnival. The girls walked around, chatting with their friends from school, riding rides, and sharing treats along the way: funnel cakes, fried Twinkies, shrimp-on-a-stick, fried pickles, and a huge lemonade to wash it all down.

By the time they met up with Trent and his friends, they were stuffed. They couldn't even think about getting on anymore rides. "Hey, baby," Trent said, kissing Marisa on the cheek.

"Hey, Trent, you working the kissing booth?" asked one of the freshmen from the cheerleading squad. "I'd pay for one of those," she said flirtatiously.

"That was downright disrespectful, Meagan," Brandi told her. She knew her from the squad, but they weren't close at all. She came across to Brandi as pushy, and her crew thought that they were better than everybody. They giggled because their leader had ruffled feathers.

Meagan was one of those freshmen who didn't know her place. She didn't care who was in a relationship when she got to PCH. If she wanted somebody, she went after them. That made her one of the most hated freshmen in her class, but she didn't seem to care about it.

Marisa wasn't bothered by Meagan, though. Trent never took his eyes off of Marisa while Meagan was obviously throwing herself at him. Marisa and Trent were in their own little world that nobody could penetrate. "Hey, don't sweat her," Marisa told Brandi, who was ready to go off on Meagan.

Ashton always knew how to break the tension. It was one of his gifts. He walked up behind Shane, grabbed her underneath her arms, and tossed her into the air. The huge lemonade she was holding wound up all over Meagan and her friends. They were as appalled and mad as a raging fire. "Yo, I'm so sorry. I had no idea that would happen," he said, stifling his laughter. The girls quickly turned and walked away.

Shane slugged Ashton for wasting their lemonade, even though she was happy it wound up all over Meagan. "People don't get mad at you, Ashton. I don't know what it is. If it was anybody else, that li'l crew probably would have attacked," Shane said.

"Girl, it's all this sex appeal. Did I tell you that I'm taking the prettiest girl in Port City to homecoming?"

"Ew, Ashton, you have to stop flirting with me," Shane squealed. "You're like my brother. Now cut it out."

"Never. You too fine to be my sister. I'm planning on making you my wife," he said, picking her up.

"Ashton, you are hopeless," Brandi said, punching him.

"Oh, you want some too, huh?" Ashton asked, chasing her and throwing her over his shoulder as he ran through the carnival.

"Stop running," he heard one of the teachers say, but he finished his circle and put her down where he found her. Brandi punched him again.

"Hey, what you doing?" she heard a familiar voice ask. It was Bryce.

"Who's this dude?" Ashton asked.

Brandi stepped in nervously. She had never seen Bryce mad before. "This is Bryce Thomas. He's my, um—"

"Boyfriend," Bryce said, looking Ashton directly in the eyes.

"Yo, dude, we cool. B is my li'l sister. That's all," Ashton told him.

Brandi couldn't believe he said that he was her boyfriend. They hadn't discussed anything like that yet, but it was kind of nice. She tried to make light of the situation. She could feel Shane and Marisa's eyes boring holes into her skin. They were both stunned. They didn't know that Brandi and Bryce had already added titles to their relationship. They had only met a couple of weeks ago, and the girls hadn't met him until now. Everyone in this group was really protective of Brandi, and Bryce was not making a good first impression.

"Well, I've heard a lot about you, Bryce. Nice to meet you," Marisa said, nudging Shane.

"Yeah, sure, what she said," Shane responded. "So, you riding with us to the dance tomorrow I hear?" she asked, looking at him like she wasn't impressed. He could feel her dislike and decided he didn't like her either.

"Yeah, I'm wit' it," he told her.

"Hey, let's go through the crazy house with all the mirrors," Brandi said, pulling him away from her group.

"That's fitting," Shane said under her breath.

Brandi turned quickly to Shane, who still wore a disapproving scowl on her face. "You behave," she mouthed to her. Shane rolled her eyes and shook her head. She loved Brandi and wasn't willing to lose her again to another psycho.

The limousine ride to the homecoming

dance turned out to be pretty awkward. With the rocky start between all of them at the carnival, being in close quarters was no day at the beach. It was Bryce who first broke the tension. "Hey, I didn't mean to come off as a jerk yesterday. I didn't know you're dating Shane," he said to Ashton.

Shane almost choked on her sparkling cider. "We are not dating."

"But you are on a date."

"Told you," Ashton said, cuddling up next to Shane. She elbowed him in the side, trying to encourage him to act appropriately. "Hey," he grimaced in pain.

"I told you, Ashton. Leave Shane alone," Trent said, laughing at his friend.

When they got to the dance, it was packed. The theme for the night was Reach for the Stars. The whole place looked like a galaxy. The blue lights danced in the dark room, which was filled with stars of various sizes. "Wow,"

Marisa said, stunned at how beautiful their cafeteria looked. "It's hard to believe that this is our lunchroom."

"It's euphoric," Shane added.

"See, man, my date got body and brains, saying all them smart people words," Ashton said, getting slugged in the arm yet again. "You can hit me if you want to. I'm never giving up on us." He batted his eyelashes at her playfully.

"Hit the floor wit' yo boy," Trent said, grabbing Marisa by the waist. Ashton and Shane followed their lead along with Brandi and Bryce. They tore up the dance floor for almost an hour. When they were done, they found a table tucked away in the corner that would give them some privacy. They were spent.

Everyone was dying of thirst by that time. So the guys volunteered to get drinks. Shane pounced on Brandi as soon as they were out of earshot. "Dude, Bryce is a'ight, but isn't he a little aggressive for you?" Shane asked, choosing her words carefully.

"No, not to me. He actually gets what I'm going through. He even talked me into going to visit my dad. It was exactly what I needed."

"I think what Shane's trying to say is that he has kind of a temper," Marisa stepped in, trying to smooth everything over.

"Well, I like him, and that's all that matters. He's good to me," she said, looking sad at the thought of her best friends not approving.

"Okay, sorry I mentioned it. If you like it, I love it," Shane told her.

By the time the guys returned with drinks, the girls wanted to go to the restroom. Shane spotted some of her photographers with their cameras and decided to stop and get some photos with her best friends. That's when she ran into Ryan, who was overseeing their work in her absence. "Thanks for stepping in for me tonight," Shane told Ryan.

"No problem," he said, looking at his feet. "So, are you having ..." his voice trailed off. Brandi had already pulled her away from him and toward the restroom. He looked like a lost puppy dog, disappointed at his prospects of finding a home.

"Sorry," she mouthed to him, tossing her dark hair over her shoulder.

After the dance, they all changed into casual clothes and headed over to Two Lanes for midnight bowling. They were staying open until four in the morning for Port City students. They had their limo until the next day and wanted to get as much use out of it as possible. They bowled until three thirty in the morning, then decided it was time to head home.

The limo driver had dropped everybody off except for Ashton and Shane. The long drive had worn her out, and she fell asleep with her head on his lap. He looked down at her and was struck by her beauty. Before they pulled onto her street, he woke her up by gently moving one of her curls that had fallen over her face.

"Are we almost there?" she asked him sleepily.

"You are so beautiful. Go back to sleep so I can look at you without you fussing at me."

She had never seen him so serious before. His eyes seemed to penetrate her soul. She was being drawn to her friend like there was a magnet between them. *What the heck?* she thought as he leaned down to kiss her. She hated crossing this line with him, but for some reason it felt right at that moment.

"Miss Foster, we're here," she heard the limo driver say.

She was breathless. "Of course, Ralphie. Thanks."

"Shane," Ashton reached out to her before she got out.

"Just leave it, Ashton." She was scared at what he would say. "Just leave it."

CHAPTER 13

Marisa

Tensions were high in the Maldonado home as they tried to prepare for Romero's court date. They didn't know what would happen. He had been charged with breaking and entering, vandalism, trespassing, possession of an illegal substance, and organized criminal activity. The whole family had been rocked to the core. What started out as a regular kid acting out, disobeying his parents, and hanging out with the wrong crowd had quickly turned into possible jail time.

Romero was not a street kid; he wasn't even street savvy. If he had been able to fool Gabino and the other guys, he definitely couldn't fool his family.

"Don't look like that," he said to Marisa, who had been quiet for most of the morning. She was already a thin girl, but she looked to be shedding weight daily.

"Like what? Like my baby brother may be going to juvie today? I feel like it's my fault. If we hadn't fought that night, you would have stayed home. I'm sorry, Rom."

"Yeah, well, I did what I did. You were trying to help me out, and I love you for it," he said, putting his head down. He knew that his actions had taken a toll on his whole family. None of his sisters attended school that day so they could support him in court. They had to show a united front in the courtroom. His attorney believed that he might get a sympathetic judge. It didn't exactly work out that way, though. He wound up in front of Judge Jellan, one of the toughest in the area. It was rumored that Judge Jellan had put his own son in jail.

When it was his turn to go before Judge Jellan, Romero thought he would die. His legs felt like spaghetti. He thought they would give out at any moment.

"Mr. Maldonado, how do you plead?" the judge asked, staring down at him.

"Not guilty, Your Honor."

Romero's family had some money, but they couldn't afford a fancy lawyer for his case. They went with the best they could afford, the Law Offices of Bruce Spencer. He allowed them to make payments instead of paying his fee up front. He wore a cheap suit and smelled like Brut cologne.

Mr. Spencer represented a lot of people in the Hispanic community. He warned the Maldonado parents that their green cards could come into question in court, but he assured them that it would just be a formality.

Romero was not impressed by his attorney, but his fate was in his hands. Attorney Spencer presented the information to the judge, but the district attorney demolished him with his evidence. It wasn't looking good for Romero.

He glanced over his shoulder at his family, who sat nervously on a wooden bench about three rows back. He couldn't believe he was here. He didn't participate in vandalizing the house. He hadn't even been the one who broke in; the Serenity they were smoking wasn't his either. Why was he the one sitting in the courtroom?

The district attorney called Mr. Maldonado to the stand. He approached the podium cautiously. He didn't know he would be called to testify against his son. He didn't want to say the wrong thing. Romero's future was hanging in the balance.

The bailiff approached the stand to conduct the swearing-in process. "I swear to tell the truth, the whole truth, and nothing but the truth," Mr. Maldonado repeated.

The district attorney started lightly with the questioning. "Sir, are you George Maldonado?"

"Yes, sir. I am."

"Mr. Maldonado, did you know that your son was involved with a known street gang, the Fifteens?"

"No, sir. To the best of my knowledge, my son is not involved with a street gang. He befriended some kids that he probably shouldn't have, but Romero is a good kid."

"Sir, good kids are at home at three a.m., not being arrested in abandoned houses, high on illegal drugs."

"Objection, Your Honor," Romero's attorney shouted, standing quickly. "That is not a question. The district attorney is on his soapbox."

"It's okay," Mr. Maldonado said. "I'd like to respond. My son was told that he was smoking a legal herb substance at the time. It was naïve and stupid, but not intentional."

"Do you always make excuses for your children, Mr. Maldonado?" asked the DA.

"Objection, Your Honor. Argumentative," Mr. Spencer jumped in.

"Sustained. Watch yourself," the judge warned the DA.

"Excuses? I'm not making excuses for him," Mr. Maldonado answered anyway, obviously frustrated by the accusation.

"Where did you think your son was at three a.m.?"

"I didn't know—"

The district attorney cut him off. "You didn't know? Do you make it a habit of not knowing where your children are?" he asked.

"Romero had been going through a lot. We were trying to give him a little space. We thought it was best."

"Do you still think that way, sir? Do

you think it wise not to keep up with your children?"

The pressure from this case was taking a toll on Mr. Maldonado. He yelled at the DA, "I know where my children are, sir. Do you always know where yours are?"

"My child is not on trial, sir. Yours is."

Mr. Maldonado stormed off the stand.

"I am not done with you, sir," the district attorney yelled. "Sit down!" But Mr. Maldonado headed toward the doors.

"George, please," he heard his wife plead from the gallery, but he could feel the heat on his neck rising out of his shirt. He couldn't seem to calm down. *How dare this man question me as a father? All that I do, I do for my children,* he thought.

"I'm going to have to ask you to take your seat at the stand, Mr. Maldonado," the judge said.

"I will not be treated like less than a man in this courtroom. The district attorney is a racist and everyone knows it."

The courtroom erupted. Many of the others awaiting trial agreed with Mr. Maldonado. Some of them even cheered. The district attorney's name was notorious in the Hispanic community, and George Maldonado was determined to stand up to him.

"I motion to hold Mr. Maldonado in contempt of court, Your Honor. At this time, I move that ICE be notified. We have evidence that Mr. Maldonado was ordered to leave the country by ICE. I believe that his green card is not valid. At this time, the Maldonado family is a burden on our society, and that burden begins with him and his son."

Mr. Maldonado lunged at the district attorney. "My family is not a burden. We work. We give back to this community. We pay taxes. I am a business owner!" he yelled as he headed toward the DA, but the bailiffs quickly stepped in and handcuffed him.

The judge picked up his gavel and beat

it hard on the desk. "Order in this court-room. Mr. Maldonado, you are being held for contempt of court. While imprisoned, US Immigration and Customs Enforce-ment will be notified to verify the validity of the DA's claims. I hope that you have all of your papers in order, or this has turned out to be a bleak day for your family."

"Papa!" Marisa shouted as he was led away by the bailiffs. Her sisters clung tightly to her.

"*Dios mio*," her mother gasped, collapsing onto the bench.

Romero never looked at his family. His head was buried in his hands. He couldn't believe what had just happened. They all knew that their father's citizenship was pending. He had taken all the right classes. Filled out all the right papers. But what would become of him now?

"Romero Maldonado, please stand."

He stood up, wiping his tear-stained face as he looked at the judge.

"Son, you brought all of this on your family, not this court. Your behavior has not only affected you but them as well, and I need you to understand that." Romero did not want to show weakness in front of the judge, but the tears would not stop. "I hereby sentence you to time served, fifty hours of community service, and a two thousand dollar fine. You are free to go at this time."

"Your Honor, may I speak?" The judge nodded his approval. "Sir, I ask that you take me and let my father out of jail. I don't want him to suffer because of my decisions."

"That is not possible, son. Your father has sealed his own fate today. The best advice I can give you is to learn your lesson from all of this. You are free to go."

When Marisa stood up, her tear-filled eyes fell directly on Trent. "What are you doing here?" she gasped.

"I thought you may need some moral support," he said.

"Well, I don't." She was embarrassed by what he had witnessed.

"Okay," he said, feeling crushed. "Do you want a ride back to school?"

"No, Trent. I'm going to be with my family today."

"I understand. Um ... I should let you go and get back to them." She watched as he walked away. She hadn't meant to hurt his feelings, but she was in shock. She had to think about her family, not him.

CHAPTER 14

Shane

There was a storm brewing inside of Shane that she couldn't calm. She was still pulling late nights with Aiden, so she was not sleeping much. Then there was the phone call; it shook her to her core. She had never heard such panic in her best friend's voice. "It didn't go well. Court was awful. They took him away, Shane. They took him away."

"Romero went back to jail?!" Her own voice began to shake as well. She could feel Marisa's pain.

"No, Romero is here. They took Papa."

"What? But why?"

"Something about the law in Texas, gangs, not having his papers ... blah, blah, blah. Papa is gone. What am I going to do? What is Mama going to do?"

"We're on our way there. We'll pick up B on the way. Sit tight."

When they arrived at the Maldonado home, everything was different. There was no soup cooking on the stove in preparation for Mr. Maldonado's arrival home from work. The small home was as clean as usual, but nothing was typical. There was no laughter, no life. It just seemed cold and empty. The head of their home was gone, and the family was frightened.

Shane and Brandi didn't know what to do. They felt like they didn't belong there during this time, like it was supposed to be a private moment for the family.

When Mrs. Maldonado came out of her room, she put all of those thoughts out of their heads. She looked like she had been crying, but she was a strong woman. She began to pull leftovers out of the refrigerator. There were homemade tamales, enchiladas, beans and rice, and tortilla soup.

She warmed everything up and made the food look like it had just been cooked. Shane stepped in and began to set the table. Marisa looked like a lost lamb. She was a daddy's girl and they knew it.

Shane and Brandi both felt guilty about eating as the Maldonados shuffled food around their plates. "This is very good, Mrs. M," Shane said, trying to break the silence.

"Gracias, Shane," she said.

Romero sat silently with his head down. "Man, I'm outta here," he stood up, frustrated.

"Mi hijo, wait." Mrs. Maldonado tried to stop him. The awkward level went up three notches at this point.

"Let him go, Mama," Marisa told her mother. "He needs some time." Nadia and Isi sat silently and watched as their family crumbled. They were too young to understand everything that was going on, but old enough to know that it wasn't good.

"You know we should be going soon too. Thank you so much for dinner," Shane said, scraping her plate.

"I'm stuffed too. Gracias, Mrs. M," Brandi told Mrs. Maldonado. She immediately began to clear the table.

"Don't touch a thing, Brandi. I need to do something to clear my mind, and cleaning this kitchen is going to be it. Go ahead and get your homework done or whatever you are going to do tonight. I love you both," she said, kissing Brandi and Shane before they left.

Marisa walked them to the front door. "Thanks, y'all, for coming over tonight," she told them.

"Just call us if you need anything," Shane told her. "We'll be right over."

By the time Shane got home from the Maldonados' house, she was spent. There were so many emotions running through her, and she still had pictures to go through and edit. It had been a long day.

"Where have you been?" Robin demanded, barging into Shane's bedroom.

"I was at Marisa's house. They are really going through a lot right now."

"Well, so am I. I count on you to be here for me, and you didn't show up. How could you?"

Shane couldn't take it anymore. She broke down and lost her cool. She started to scream at her sister; something that she didn't do often. "I'm not your lifeline, Robin. I can't schedule my life around yours and Aiden's needs. I'm a teenager. I'm not the one who had a baby. You are!" she yelled.

Her mother came upstairs when she heard all of the commotion. "Are you okay, Shane?" she asked.

"No, I'm not okay," Shane snapped at her. "I'm angry at both of you. Shoot, I'm angry with Grandma too for making you as selfish as you are, Mom. How dare you not help your daughter with her child?" she scolded her mother.

"Shane, don't you speak to me that way," her mother said, trying not to lose her temper.

"I will," Shane told her, "because some-body has to tell you that you are wrong. And, Robin, I love you, and I love Aiden, but I can't make up for all the help that you are not getting from Mom or from Gavin. I can't make up for everybody else."

"But you are all I have," Robin said through her tears. "Sometimes I just look forward to taking a shower, washing my hair, something normal," she sobbed.

"Sissy, you know I'll still be here for

you, but I need help too. Neither one of us is getting any sleep. All of our free time is spent taking care of Aiden. Shoot, look at your toes. The chipped polish says it all."

"Shut up, Shane," she said, nudging her sister. The tears fell from her eyes like they had lost the fight against gravity.

"What, Robin? What?"

"I don't think I can do this anymore. I don't really know what to do. I really messed up my life. I mean, I wouldn't trade my little guy for anything, but I wasn't ready for all of this."

Her mother turned to leave, and Shane lost it.

"How can you walk out on your daughters? We are telling you that we are struggling, and you don't even care. You don't work, Mom. You never did. Don't act like you are so strong and independent. You sit around waiting for Dad to give you money and take care of you."

"You are on thin ice, Shane. You better

watch it. You don't know what I have sacrificed for the two of you. I had dreams too, but I put them on hold because I was a mother first, and that's what Robin is going to have to do too."

"Is that really what you want for her, Mom? You want her to be dependent on a man just like you?"

That was the last thing Mrs. Foster wanted for her daughter. She knew the sacrifice that went along with being dependent on anybody for anything, but admitting that she was wrong was never her strength.

"Look, I did the best I could when I had Robin. My mom didn't help me, and it made me stronger. If Grandma had held my hand through every little thing, I wouldn't be the woman I am today."

"Is that how you rationalize walking by me like nothing's going on when you see me struggling?" Robin asked her mother. She shook her head in disbelief. "All this time, I thought that you were mad at me for getting pregnant, for embarrassing you and Dad, so I never asked you for any help."

"Embarrassed? Baby, I'm not embarrassed by you or Aiden. I was practicing tough love. I thought I was helping you. You need to toughen up now that you're a mother."

"Mom, you couldn't have thought that." Robin couldn't seem to stop crying. "This has been the hardest thing I've ever done in my life, and you abandoned me. One thing that you have taught me is to never make this mistake with my daughter. If she would have me, I'd be by her side every step of the way."

"I hope you're not saying that you condone teenage pregnancy, Robin. Because that's the last thing I would support. You now know how impossibly hard it is to take care of an infant."

Aiden began to cry right along with

his mother. It was time for her to get back to him. She moved in the direction of the door, looking spent and overwhelmed.

"Wait, honey. I'll get Aiden."

"You will?" Shane said, surprised.

"Yeah, and I'll start helping you out a little. I don't have to be my mother. I'm sorry that I haven't been helping at all," she said, hugging her oldest daughter.

"Mama wasn't there for me because she felt as though I tainted the family by marrying a black man. But listen, Robin, you did this to yourself. We give you food and shelter. Having a baby at your age was the last thing we wanted for you. But we supported your decision."

Aiden let out another big cry. "Grand is coming, Aiden. Give me one sec. I'll help you with Aiden, but you are his mother. And he is your primary responsibility," she lectured. "Now I am going to go get that precious boy."

Robin fell onto Shane's bed in tears.

"It's been so much, Shane. I feel like a huge weight has been lifted off of my shoulders."

Shane rubbed her sister's back while she cried. "It's okay, Robin. It's going to be okay."

Shane left her bedroom in a much better mood and went looking for her father.

"Dad, we need to talk," Shane said, walking into her father's downstairs office.

"Hey, baby girl. What's on your mind?" her father asked.

"Everything is on my mind. Do you know what happened to the Maldonados?"

"Yeah, your mother filled me in on everything. She is very upset."

"I never ask you for help for my friends, but I have to ask for it now. They need your help."

"I can't really get involved with anything like that, Shane. George is an awesome guy, but immigration is a touchy topic, not only in Port City but in the country."

"But, Dad, who else can help Mr. M?"

Mr. Foster worked for the city directly under the city manager. He had friends in high places, but he wasn't one to ask for favors. He didn't even ask for favors when his own daughters were in trouble, much less their friends. Actually, he had already tried to find out some information on the Maldonado case when his wife first told him about it. What he discovered was that the DA was adamant about making Mr. Maldonado pay for disrespecting him in court. Mr. Foster had felt so much tension from just asking questions, he had dropped it. But now that his baby girl sat in his office pleading with him, he knew he had to do something.

"Listen, I'll see what I can do. I'm going to talk to George soon, and I'm going to make some calls. I can't make any promises about the outcome, but this is going to be my top priority. Now stop worrying." He stood up from behind his desk to give his daughter a hug. "How's your sister doing? I heard a lot of drama going on upstairs."

"She's getting better. Pregnancy and then labor, it was hard on her. I've been trying to help."

"I know you have. But Aiden is your sister's responsibility. You are a great sister, Shane. And I am proud of you."

"Thanks, Dad, for everything," she told him, standing on her toes to give him a kiss on the cheek. He could always make her feel like a little girl. She lived for that man. He was so strong and smart; everything a father should be.

CHAPTER 15

Brandi

Come in, come in," Mrs. Haywood said to Bryce as he stood on the porch wiping his feet on the welcome mat. "Get out of that cold and rain. Would you like something warm to drink?" she asked him.

"Nah, I'm good," he told her. She was used to Brandi being around kids who said ma'am when they spoke to adults. He had caught her a little off guard.

"Brandi!" she yelled. "Your friend is here." She sat down with Bryce while he waited for Brandi. In the past, she would have stayed out of Brandi's way and let her make her own decisions when dating. But after her abduction, Mrs. Haywood thought it might be a good idea to be more hands-on in Brandi's social life. "So, tell me a little bit about yourself, Bryce."

"Not much to tell. I'm trying to make it out here on my own. But at the same time I'm trying to take care of my mom."

"What does your mother do?" she asked.

"Oh, nothing. She's a drug addict like your husband. Holding down a job is kind of difficult for her."

"Oh, I see." Brandi had not mentioned to Mrs. Haywood that Bryce's mother was an addict. She didn't have anything against him for that. She knew that problems within a family could cause problems within an individual. Mrs. Haywood wanted her daughter to have a stress free teenage life, not one filled with addicts. One was enough.

Brandi came bolting down the stairs as

soon as she was done getting ready. They planned to kick back and watch a movie. The weather was getting worse by the minute, and even though it was daytime, there was barely any sun outside. "Hey, Bryce," she said, giving him a big hug that was not lost on her mother.

"I'm going to go and get candles ready in case the lights go out," Mrs. Haywood told them. "Let me know if you all need anything."

"Your mom is nice," Bryce told Brandi.

"Yeah, she's a lot more involved with me now. I guess she doesn't have to focus all of her attention on my dad since he's in rehab."

"Yeah, I bet. You wanna download a movie. My grandmother is scared to drive in bad weather, so I'm not sure how long I can stay."

"I'm sure my mom won't mind driving you home."

"All right!" Brandi's sister, Raven, chirped

as she hopped down the stairs. "What movie are we watching?"

"You are not watching anything," Brandi told her.

"Uh-huh, I'll go make the popcorn." Raven ran to make the snack.

"Sorry about that," Brandi told him, but he shrugged it off.

They decided to watch the original *Nightmare on Elm Street*. The darkness of the sky and the cold temperature mixed with the sound of the rain made it a perfect day for scary movies. Raven was screaming and burying her face in her sister's arm. By the time they made it to *Nightmare on Elm Street 3*, they had lost Raven. She was no longer interested in watching movies, especially scary ones. Their date seemed to fly by. They had fun together. It seemed easy and carefree.

"What are you doing tomorrow?" he asked her.

"I have to spend some time with Marisa

and her family. They are going through a rough patch."

"So am I. What about me?" he asked. Brandi didn't know if he was joking or not. She didn't know how to respond.

"What about you?" she asked, speaking slowly.

"You need to be worried about me. I'm your boyfriend. You know that my mom is not doing well. Nah, you ain't got time to go to Marisa's at all."

Brandi looked confused. "Mari is my best friend, and I'm going to be there for her. My friends are my family. You know they saved my life last year. I probably wouldn't even be here if it weren't for them."

"Fine, do what you want, but don't call me when you're done."

"That's not fair, Bryce."

"Life ain't fair. Haven't you learned that?"

He was turning their fun date into an

argument, and Brandi wasn't in the mood. She wanted to put some space between them. "Hey, you 'bout ready to roll out? I'm going to tell my mom."

"Oh, so now you trying to get rid of me?" he asked, stepping closer to her face.

"No," she said, afraid of how he would act if she told the truth.

"Everything okay in here?" her mother asked, seeing how close they were.

"Yeah, Mom, we are good. Can you drive Bryce home please?"

Brandi could tell that Bryce was still angry, but she didn't care. She'd had enough of trying to make other people happy.

After the Haywoods dropped Bryce home, Mrs. Haywood felt like she should talk to her daughter about her relationship. The drive home was as good a time as any.

"B, can I ask you something?"

"Of course, Mom." Their relationship was so much better than before. Her mom was really trying to be involved in her life, and it was kind of nice.

"Do you think it's a good idea to be in a relationship right now?"

"I'm fine, Mom. Don't worry about me."

"It's not you I'm worried about so much. I wonder if Bryce is carrying too much on his shoulders to be the right person for you."

"You can't judge him for what his mom is, just like people shouldn't judge me for the decisions that Dad's made. Mom, he's the only person who understands. Our parents' addictions make us different from everybody else. He gets my pain."

"Okay, baby. Just be careful. You and your sister are all I have in this world."

"I know, Mom. I will."

CHAPTER 16

A Holiday Wish

As the Maldonados gathered around the table at the Fosters' home for Thanksgiving, the mood was solemn. Mrs. Maldonado had not been in the right frame of mind to cook her usual Thanksgiving meal with her husband locked away. It had been weeks since the trial landed Mr. Maldonado in jail. She had gone to visit a remorseful George a week after the trial. "*Lo siento,*" he kept saying, apologizing for how he had behaved in court. "This is all my fault."

"We are going to get through this. I promise we will." It was all she could say to try to keep his spirits up. She wished that he was home to encourage her a little bit too. The money that they did have was drying up. Their family counted on Mr. Maldonado's construction business to bring in income, and things weren't running smoothly without him overseeing it. They didn't know how much longer his business would survive.

"Okay, okay, it's time to say grace," Mr. Foster said, carrying the huge turkey that he'd carved in the kitchen only minutes before. The holiday table was an impressive sight! Between Mrs. Maldonado and Mrs. Foster, they had covered all the bases. There was the traditional Thanksgiving meal of turkey, ham, cornbread dressing, rice dressing, macaroni and cheese, potato salad, green bean casserole, and cranberry sauce; then there was the Mexican food that was just as mouth-watering: tamales, enchiladas, tortilla soup, guacamole, and homemade salsa. The dessert table was filled with pecan and sweet potato pies, Italian cream cake, *tres leches* cake, and a two-layer flan.

Mr. Foster led them in prayer. "Lord, thank you for this wonderful meal. Thank you for our extended family joining us for Thanksgiving this year. We ask you today to bring closure to their situation, and bring George home where he belongs. We thank you for your grace and mercy, because we need plenty of it. Thank you for all that you have done in each of our lives. May we continue to be a blessing to others. Amen."

"Amen," the two families said in unison.

After thirty minutes of filling up on the food, everybody was ready to start tearing into the dessert table. "You are barely eating, Lupe," Mrs. Foster told Mrs. Maldonado.

"Kim, I don't have an appetite with George gone. He is my entire life, you know?"

"I know, but I'm sure everything will be fine." The ladies began to clean up while the kids all sat around talking. Soon everyone was engrossed in the Denzel Washington movie that came out on DVD in time for Thanksgiving.

"You should stay here tonight," Shane told Marisa.

"No, I can't leave my family tonight. We all miss Papa so much, and he's calling tonight. I have to be home for that."

"I understand. Have you talked to Trent?"

"No, not today," she said, lowering her head. "I was really rude to him when he came to court, and things haven't been the same since then. I haven't been the same since then. Maybe I'm not in a good place to be in a relationship right now. I don't know."

"Hey, when your dad gets home, your world is going to get back to normal. I'm sure Trent will understand that it was just a rough patch for you."

"I don't know if my dad is coming home, Shane. I'm starting to wonder. We all thought that he would be home by Thanksgiving, but that hasn't happened."

"Look, my dad has been calling in some favors. I know he's working overtime on your father's case."

"I don't want your father to do that."

"What are friends for if they can't help you out when you are in need?"

After Thanksgiving break was over, nobody was in the mood to go back to school. Teachers and students looked like zombies after the long holiday, and trying to do homework seemed almost pointless. The smarter teachers gave hands-on assignments that made class a little more tolerable, but the other teachers either lectured or gave reading assignments that made class drag by for them and their students.

The only thing that could bring a smile to everyone's face was the mention of Christmas break. The fall decorations in the hallways had already morphed into Christmas trees, snowflakes, and all things winter. When teachers had time to magically change decorations was still lost on the students, but they always seemed to get it done.

After school, Brandi, Shane, and Marisa stood close to the journalism room waiting for Mrs. Monroe to show up. They wanted to talk to her about Marisa's dad. She was always a good sounding board for their problems. Instead of Mrs. Monroe, Ryan showed up with her keys and let himself into her classroom. They were right behind him.

"Where's Mrs. Monroe? Is she coming?" Shane asked.

"She said she had a faculty meeting, but I'm sure she'll be here at some point. She has to get her keys. How was Thanksgiving?" he asked, looking only at Shane.

"It was good. Yours?"

"Somebody has a *crush*," Brandi said, getting quickly punched by Shane.

"Good. I mean Thanksgiving was good." Ryan became flustered at the exchange. Talking to girls had always been difficult for him, but when he looked at Shane, it was even harder.

"Hey, you know what? We'll try to catch Mrs. Monroe tomorrow."

"Okay. I'll tell her you stopped by."

Marisa was distraught. "I just wanted to talk to her. She can always make me feel better."

As they turned the corner close to the gym, they could see Trent digging through his locker. "Big T!" Shane yelled as they were walking up. He turned quickly to see who had called his name, and that's when

Ashley came into view. She was leaning against the lockers, smiling up at Trent. A blind person could see that Ashley was shamelessly flirting with him, and the bad thing was that he looked like he was enjoying it.

That moment was too much for Marisa. Her world was closing in on her, and she needed to put some space between herself and her problems, so she turned and ran. "Mari!" she heard Trent yell, but she kept on going.

"Great, Trent," Brandi snapped.

"Skank," Shane said, turning her frustration on Ashley. "Come on, B, let's go find Mari," she said, rolling her eyes at Trent.

When they finally found Marisa, she had already made it home. She didn't let them in when they stopped by, which was totally unlike her. Mrs. Maldonado told them that Marisa didn't want to see anybody. It remained that way for the next few weeks. She withdrew. Nobody could reach her. She was at school, but she wasn't there. She wouldn't even speak to Trent. Between her father, her brother, and Trent, she felt like the men in her life were letting her down.

By the time Christmas break began, she was barely talking to Shane or Brandi either. Shane kept trying to reassure her that Mr. Foster was going to be able to help, but Marisa was losing faith. "Nobody can help us."

Her father called the house from time-to-time, but she was angry with him too. He had always told her to keep her cool and make smart moves, but he hadn't taken his own advice. Now look where they were.

On Christmas Eve, the Maldonados and the Haywoods joined the Fosters at their home for eggnog, appetizers, and caroling, but none of their fathers were present. They all had some excuse as to why they couldn't spend Christmas Eve with their families. Mr. Maldonado was in jail; Mr. Haywood was still in rehab; Mr. Foster was MIA. "I hate this stupid tradition," Marisa blurted out during "Jingle Bells." She threw the Santa hat she was wearing on the ground.

"Mi hija!" Mrs. Maldonado scolded her. "We are guests in this home. You will not behave this way. It's Christmas."

"Well, I can't pretend to be happy ... Christmas or not. I'm outta here."

When the door swung open, there was a surprise on the other side. Mr. Maldonado was walking up the sidewalk just in time.

"Papa!" Marisa screamed. His other children ran to see what she was yelling about. Mrs. Maldonado waited patiently as she watched her husband with his children. His absence had taken a toll on all of them, but here he was.

"You're here, but how?" Mrs. Maldonado said softly.

"You can thank Brian for that. I don't know how he did it, but he got me home by Christmas like he promised."

"Well, I had to make a few promises of my own to some pretty important people, but we'll talk about it later," Mr. Foster said, looking at his wife.

Nobody noticed another figure coming up the driveway. "Hey, is my family in here?" James Haywood asked, knocking on the opened door.

"Daddy!" Raven yelled, jumping on him.

"Hey, Dad," Brandi said, giving her father a hug and kissing his cheek. "Mr. Maldonado just came home too. This is awesome. How did you get here?"

"I've been on the bus all day. I didn't want to bother any of you, and you know they wouldn't let me drive. It doesn't matter how I got here, though. Just know Daddy's happy to be home."

Marisa was still overwhelmed. She

couldn't believe that her dad was really with her. She was still skeptical. "Dad, are you back for good?" she asked, still looking shocked.

In Mr. Maldonado's hand was a sheet of paper, he asked for everyone's attention. "Not only have all the charges been dropped against me, but they put a rush on my paperwork. I get sworn in on the first day that the courts open back up after the holidays."

They all began to celebrate. "Wait, wait, *espera* ... that's not the best part. *Mi amor*, you get sworn in on the same day with me. We will both be US citizens in less than two weeks."

"Dios mio," Mrs. Maldonado said, not believing her ears. She grabbed her husband gently by the face and kissed him. "This is unreal. How can we ever thank you, Brian? We've had a green card for so long, but I never thought—"

"Well, since you asked. One of the promises I had to make was to represent our neighborhood in the election next year. I'm running for city council for the ninth precinct."

Nobody knew what to say.

It was Mrs. Maldonado who broke the ice. "Well, Councilman, sounds like we'll be raising money next year. You can count on me to cook lots of tamales."

"Congratulations, Brian, you know you have my support. Anything you need, man," Mr. Haywood told him.

"Kim, you still thinking?" he asked his wife.

"I'm with you one hundred percent," she said, kissing him on the lips.

"Shane? Robin?"

"Sure, Dad," Shane said nervously. She wasn't sure if she was ready for all of this, but if everyone else was willing, then who was she to complain?

"They are going to try to demolish me in the press, Dad. I know it," Robin said, balancing Aiden in her arms.

"They better not. My family is off limits," he promised.

Marisa sat tucked under her dad's arm, not wanting to ever move again. "This has been the best Christmas Eve ever," she declared. It looked like Romero was having a difficult time adjusting. He had yet to say a word. As soon as Marisa could grab him, she did.

"What's wrong, Romero?" she asked, following him outside.

"It was all my fault, all of this. I'm relieved, of course. I think Dad hates me, though."

"I could never hate you," their father said, joining them outside. "If my dad hated me for all that I did growing up, we wouldn't have a relationship today. It's okay, son. We all make mistakes. Just don't make the same ones again."

"I won't, Dad. I promise."

When their father was gone, it was as if they were in the middle of a violent storm. Now it was just the opposite. There was calm, peace, and hope for a very bright future.

New Beginnings

Their traditional New Year's party had not been planned this year. With the absence of Mr. Maldonado and Mr. Haywood, it hadn't seemed right. Now that they were both back home, the girls thought a celebration was required.

The New Year's party that usually took months to plan had been thrown together in a week. The food had been the easy part, but the accessories that normally gave it that extra pizzazz had been hard to come by. The girls took to the Internet to try and help their mothers with the decorations. They were getting older and wanted to be more hands-on. After all, their parents were doing this for them. What better way to show their appreciation?

Brandi had found a cool new website that had great DIY ideas. Instead of buying the New Year's number signs, they made them from cardboard and left-over Christmas garland. They used the computer to make Happy New Year decals to go over the pastries wrapped in plastic.

They took regular black birthday hats and added cute little clocks with hands that pointed toward midnight. They used silver and gold Mardi Gras beads that they had saved. Luckily they were able to find noisemakers in the same color. There was no way they were making those.

They even decorated the backyard with Christmas lights and turned on the fire pit to keep it toasty. Most of the decorations were handmade and inexpensive. They were proud of their work when they were done.

The night of the party, there was so much to be optimistic about. The Fosters were moving into a new chapter of their lives with the upcoming campaign. The Haywood girls were happy for their father's recovery and completion of rehab. The Maldonado parents were about to become US citizens. What could be better than that? The lightheartedness of the evening was irreplaceable and definitely needed.

The doorbell rang, and Shane hopped up to answer it. "Hey, I think somebody wants to see you," she told Marisa.

When Marisa looked up, she saw Trent looking down at her. "Can we talk?" he asked. He led her into the den that was rarely used by the Foster family. "Look, I don't know what we are doing here, but

I miss—" Before he could complete his sentence, she reached up and kissed him.

"I'm sorry. I couldn't get my thoughts straight. It was all—"

"Shhh," he said, kissing her again. "It doesn't even matter anymore. None of it does."

Marisa knew he was right. It was all good, and she didn't mind at all. "Now let's get back to the party." They walked out hand in hand.

"Now that's what I like to see," Ashton said, sitting next to Shane near the fireplace.

"I'm going to get something to drink. Anybody need anything?" Shane asked. They all declined the offer. When Shane got close to the door, the bell rang again. There stood Ryan Petry, his light skin complementing the brown peacoat he wore. For some girls, he was dreamy and sophisticated, but Shane found him a bit too serious. He reminded her of her father.

"Well, I didn't think that you would make it," she said. "Come in. The rest of the journalism class is hanging out in the living room with Mrs. Monroe, but you are welcome to roam. There is a fire going, so go get warm."

"Thanks," he said. He noticed her moving in the opposite direction and followed her lead toward the kitchen. "Hey, can I get a minute with you before we meet up with everyone?"

"Yeah, let's go to my dad's office," she said, guiding him through the crowded house.

"Look, I don't want it to be awkward between us if I'm honest with you."

"Okay, you're scaring me. What's on your mind?"

"I ..." He stopped. "I'm so nervous," he admitted. "I don't know why you have this effect on me. I usually pride myself on finding the right words. Okay, here goes ... simply put, I would love to take you out sometime," he said, taking a deep breath.

Shane laughed. She couldn't believe he was that nervous to ask her out. "You know what?" she said, giving it some thought. "I'd like that. Let's do it before we go back to school. This is the only free time we'll have."

"Well, that was less painful than I thought," he said, breathing a sigh of relief.

"Come on. Let's get you some food and a drink. It's getting close to midnight."

At eleven thirty, everyone started writing down their hopes for the year to come. They placed them in a balloon and filled the balloon with helium. By the time each person completed their balloons and loaded up on New Year's noisemakers, hats, and beads, there was only five minutes to go. They all gathered in the backyard, ready to launch their balloons and send their New Year's wishes to the heavens.

"Okay, okay, everybody get ready!" Mr. Foster shouted.

"Ten, nine, eight, seven, six, five, four, three, two, one! Happy New Year!" They sent their silver balloons soaring through the night sky. The balloons danced and mixed with the fireworks that shone brilliantly in the darkness.

"Now this is what New Year's is supposed to be like," Bryce said, looking at Brandi lovingly.

"I'm glad you're here," she told him.

"Me too."

Ashton looked at Shane as she swept her nephew up into her arms. He loved what he saw. She was everything that a guy could want, if only she could take him seriously. She acted like the kiss they shared didn't exist, and she refused to talk about it.

She was his New Year's wish. She just didn't know it. Ryan's eyes were glued to her too. She had two admirers, but Shane was being Shane and having fun. Nobody could tie her down, which was probably why they both wanted to.

The girls always found a way to sneak away from the excitement of the party to spend a few minutes together. As they gathered in Shane's room to look over the past year, they realized the journey they had been on.

"If I have to be on this ride, I'm glad I'm on it with the two of you," Marisa told them.

"Me too," Brandi said.

"I wouldn't have it any other way," Shane declared, giving her best friends a tight hug.

Their embrace seemed to squeeze the past year away and make room for the year to come. They had all survived and were better off because of it. All of the drama, tears, and heartache made them smarter, stronger, and wiser. Who could ask for more?

ABOUT THE AUTHOR

Shannon Freeman

Born and raised in Port Arthur, Texas, Shannon Freeman works full time as an English teacher in her hometown. After completing college at Oral Roberts University, Freeman began her work in the classroom teaching English and oral communications. At that time, the characters of her breakout series, Port City High, began to form, but these characters would not come to life for years. An apartment fire destroyed almost all of the young teacher's worldly possessions before she could begin writing. With nothing to lose, Freeman packed up and headed to Los Angeles, California, to pursue a passion that burned within her since her youth, the entertainment industry.

Beginning in 2001, Freeman made numerous television appearances and enjoyed a rich life full of friends and hard work. In 2008, her world once again changed when she and her husband, Derrick Freeman, found out that they were expecting their first child. Freeman then made the difficult decision to return to Port Arthur and start the family that she had always wanted.

At that time, Freeman returned to the classroom, but entertaining others was still a desire that could not be quenched. Being in the classroom again inspired her to tell the story of Marisa, Shane, and

Brandi that had been evolving for almost a decade. She began to write and the Port City High series was born.

Port City High is the culmination of Freeman's life experiences, including her travels across the United States and Europe. Her stories reflect the friendships she's made across the globe. Port City High is the next breakout series for today's young adult readers. Freeman says, "The topics are relevant and life changing. I just hope that people are touched by my characters' stories as much as I am."